KISSING on THIRD

KISSING on THIRD

Heather B. Moore
Rebecca Connolly
Sophia Summers

Mirror Press

Copyright © 2019 by Heather B. Moore
Print edition
All rights reserved

No part of this book may be reproduced in any form whatsoever without prior written permission of the publisher, except in the case of brief passages embodied in critical reviews and articles. This is a work of fiction. The characters, names, incidents, places, and dialogue are products of the author's imagination and are not to be construed as real.

Interior design by Cora Johnson
Edited by Kelsey Down and Lisa Shepherd
Cover design by Rachael Anderson
Cover image credit: Deposit Photos #38601475
Published by Mirror Press, LLC
ISBN: 978-1-947152-64-9

Belltown Six Pack Series

Hitching the Pitcher
Falling for Centerfield
Charming the Shortstop
Snatching the Catcher
Flirting with First
Kissing on Third

Kissing on Third

His past will never go away. Hers has left deep scars. Together, maybe they can build something new.

Levi Cox carved his baseball game out of the dirt. The hard way. Bouncing between foster homes as a kid, and trying everything he could do to protect his kid brother from bullies, Levi backs down from no one and has a record to prove it. Baseball has given him a purpose and a career. A way to provide for his brother. When Levi meets Finley Gray, he finds things happening to his heart that he never thought possible. She has her own broken past, using boxing as her outlet. Yet the more Levi gets to know Finley, the more he's convinced they belong together. Breaking through Finley's tough exterior might be Levi's hardest challenge ever. But he has a feeling it will be more than worth it.

CHAPTER 1

"I'M SORRY . . . BRANDY . . . I'm not available after the game." Levi Cox inched away from the woman with the huge blue eyes who was looking at him like she was a stray dog and he was her first meal in a week. Her grip on his arm only tightened.

"Brindy," she said, her voice breathless, screechy, and, well, annoying. "Kind of like Brandy, but with an *i*, although it sounds like an *e*."

The red of her lipstick had smeared on her teeth. Should Levi tell her? Would it be polite or rude?

"Well, you've got my number, Levi Cox," Brandy-Brindy-Brendy continued.

"I sure do."

She laughed. High. Giggly.

Levi winced. She'd latched onto him as he walked from the parking lot to the stadium, and in a move that would impress any baseball coach, she had grasped his arm and written seven numbers on his skin with a purple Sharpie.

Levi had been too stunned to pull his arm away.

She was a tiny thing, harmless enough, right? But now he

wasn't so sure. Her blue eyes seemed darkly beady now, like a ferret, and her rather long fingernails were digging into his arm. Where were his teammates? He was early, but not that early. Someone from the Minnesota Ice should be here. But no one seemed to be around except for Ferret Lady.

His phone rang. Levi normally sent calls to voicemail unless it was Coach. "Sorry, gotta run." He pretty much tore his arm away from the woman, then strode toward the stadium. She called after him, but he'd already answered his phone like he'd been thrown a lifeline.

"Rabbit," Levi said. "I owe you."

"You got that right," Ryker Stone, a.k.a. Rabbit, said. "Losers always buy dinner."

"I'm not talking about betting on tonight's game," Levi said. "I was being accosted by a rabid female in the parking lot who wrote her phone number on my arm with a purple Sharpie. Your phone call gave me the perfect getaway."

Rabbit laughed.

"Not funny."

Rabbit kept laughing. "If you can't fend off a starry-eyed fan, you're definitely going to get crushed tonight. The Minnesota Ice are going dowwwwn, baby."

Levi yanked open the team-only door to the stadium. "You won't even get on third base, so get ready to give your team a pep talk after you lose."

Rabbit chuckled. "Don't you ever watch the press? We're picked to win, and I couldn't agree more."

Levi never watched the press. He didn't want to be a headcase like some players he knew who obsessively watched film and newscasts. No, Levi didn't have time for that stuff. If he wasn't working out, in practice, or at a game, he would go spend time with his little brother. It kept them both out of trouble.

"You still there?" Rabbit asked.

"Yeah, just got to the locker room," he said. "Gotta go."

"Wait," Rabbit said. "The guys want to go out tonight, you know, see the nightlife in Minneapolis."

Levi paused at his locker. "The guys? As in your Baltimore Blue Jay teammates?"

"Yeah. So? Are you up for it? Don't tell me you're afraid of a few Blue Jays."

Levi scoffed and opened his locker. "I'm not playing party host. I'm flying out early to see Rhett."

"Cool," Rabbit said. "How's he doing?"

"Stressed," Levi said. "Summer school in college is more intense."

"True," Rabbit said. "Tonight's game should be over by nine. We go hit a restaurant. You'll be home in your comfy bed by eleven. How about it?"

"I don't think so," Levi said. "There's too many variables."

"Like what?"

Levi sighed. "You know. It's better if I stay away from the whole bar scene."

"It doesn't have to be a bar."

"Tell that to the Blue Jays," Levi said. "Look, man, it will be good to see you, but I'm outta here after the game."

Rabbit protested again, but Levi cut him off. "Gotta go, man. See you in a few hours."

Levi hung up, then set his stuff in the locker. He'd come early to work on some cardio and weights. On game days, he was always more limber and played better if he did a workout in the team's weight room a few hours before. Some might call it overkill, but it paid off for Levi.

It also helped settle his nerves.

He'd been playing third base for the Minnesota Ice pro

baseball team for four years now. He and five of his college teammates from Belltown University in Western Massachusetts had all been called up to the Major Leagues the same year, after winning the NCAA championship for the third year in a row. The media had been crazy, and the teammates had been dubbed the Belltown Six Pack. Six players, six best friends, all called up.

Rabbit played first base for the Baltimore Blue Jays; David McCarthy—Grizz—played catcher for the Pittsburgh Knights; Sawyer Bennett, a.k.a. Skeeter, pitched for the Columbus Black Racers; Axel Diaz—the Axe Man—played shortstop for the Seattle Sharks; and finally, Cole Hunter—Big Dawg—played centerfield for the Los Angeles Sea Rays.

They were Levi's family. The only family he'd ever had except for his younger half-brother, who was now in college—and Levi was damn proud of the kid. They'd come from nothing. Literally. Mom in jail, both dads gone. It wasn't until Levi's sophomore year in high school that he found baseball, or more accurately, baseball found him.

Levi had been at his umpteenth foster home with his younger brother. Rhett was one of those kids who got picked on. Yeah, he was skinny, undersized, but there was no sign on him that said *Bully me.* The only thing Levi could figure was that Rhett just had a brain and used it. He wasn't afraid to answer the teachers' questions, and Rhett always got them right. He could remember anything he read. In short, he was brilliant.

Levi wasn't. But he could hold his own with any bully, especially when Rhett refused to defend himself. He took whatever people dished out, didn't fight back. It drove Levi nuts, but the problem was, his brother was four years younger than him, so they were never in the same school together.

Levi had been enrolled in his fourth high school when his

foster mom had texted him that Rhett had been shoved inside a locker by some other kids at the middle school.

Levi saw the text when he was heading back from the track during PE. When he got to the high school locker rooms, his anger exploded at thinking of his little brother stuck inside a locker. Levi had grabbed a bat from the PE bin and swung it at the set of lockers. Over and over.

When he finished, he found that he had an audience. The high school baseball coach.

"Well, son," Coach Reed had said. "If you can swing that hard, might as well try it on a baseball."

The memory of those days was both dark and painful, yet Coach Reed had become the one burning light in Levi's life. And Levi credited baseball as the reason he didn't end up living the rest of his teenage years on the streets or in juvie. And the reason he could now fully pay for his brother's living expenses and schooling.

Levi put in his earbuds, cranked up the music, and walked into the team training room. He'd run a couple of miles on the treadmill, then hit the free weights. His normal routine took about an hour and a half. He'd finish off with a series of stretches before hitting the batting cage.

Today was no different. When he reached the cool-down phase, he took out his ear buds and wiped off his face with a towel. Out of the corner of his eye, he saw someone step into the training room.

"Thought I'd find you here."

Levi spun. Ryker Stone leaned against the wall, his arms folded, his white-blond hair a messy mop on his head, his blue eyes intent on Levi.

"Rabbit! Decided to put in some real man hours?"

Rabbit laughed. "You know I could outrun you any day."

Levi grinned and walked toward Rabbit. They gripped

hands. None of the Six Pack tried to hug Levi, and he was good with that. Besides, he was soaked in sweat right now, so he was sure Rabbit appreciated it as well.

"I'm ready to go, if you are," Levi said. "First one across the field and back gets a hundred bucks."

Rabbit lifted his brows. "That's pocket change to you, Steal. Word is that you've got a nest egg saved since you refuse to upgrade your 1989 Bronco and have yet to buy a couch."

"Who told you about my non-couch?"

"Grizz—"

"You can't believe everything Grizz says," Levi cut in. "But I'll raise you two hundred dollars if that makes you feel better."

"Now you're talking," Rabbit said. "Either that or you're wrongfully confident."

Levi tugged off his shirt and tossed it on a bench. "Let's go now."

So the two men strode to the empty baseball field.

"Thought you said Minnesota was cold," Rabbit said.

"It's *July*," Levi said. "Come back in January."

Rabbit smirked, then stopped near the home plate. "Ready?"

"Yep."

They ran, sprinting side by side until they reached the top of centerfield. Rabbit hit the backboard two seconds before Levi. But Levi wasn't going to let up, and as he turned to head back to home plate, he lengthened his stride and caught up. They crossed the baseline at the same time. Without a witness, it was impossible to say who'd been a fraction of an inch in front.

"Tied!" Rabbit whooped, then bent over, placing his hands on his knees as he gulped in air.

Levi walked in small circles, cooling down his body. "Let's go again."

Rabbit laughed. "You're nuts."

The two men took off again. But the second race ended in another tie.

"Okay, okay," Rabbit said, panting. "I think we're going to have to come up with another bet that can't possibly end in a tie. Whoever steals the most bases tonight chooses the location for dinner. Whoever steals the fewest pays the tab."

Levi scrubbed a hand through his hair and groaned. "I'm so going to regret this."

Rabbit only grinned. "Well, your nickname is Steal for a reason. Time to show the Blue Jays your stuff."

Chapter 2

"Put 'em in Finley's section."

"What the heck?" Finley whirled to face her boss. Mark's flyaway eyebrows were raised, as if he was waiting for her to argue.

But Finley couldn't argue, not if she wanted to keep her job. She was supposed to be off in twenty minutes. Now it would be more like forty if she had to wait on a table of six people. She was depending on the extra time to get ready for the fight tonight. She felt good, strong, ready, but she needed to spend time visualizing the boxing match against Star. Finley had been training diligently since their last fight that she'd lost. With the extra conditioning, she knew she had a chance. Plus, the pot was $500. Money she could sorely use.

She eyed the group of guys heading over to her section. Jess, the hostess of the Green Falcon Irish Pub, scooted a couple of the tables together so the six men could sit together. Two of the men helped, grinning at Jess and her rather large display of bosom. Jess only giggled.

Great.

Kissing on Third

Jess used to work at Hooters and still dressed like it.

The six guys were baseball players by the looks of their matching Blue Jays ball caps. All except one, who wasn't wearing a hat. His dirty-blond hair was kind of messy, and it looked like he hadn't shaved for a couple of days. Finley had a feeling that was his usual look, since he didn't seem to be the type of guy to put a lot of primping into his appearance. He wore a leather jacket that had seen better days, along with worn jeans—ones that were truly worn and not purchased that way.

Finley averted her gaze. Checking out baseball guys wouldn't take her anyplace good tonight. She had to keep her mind focused, not thinking about how, according to her boss Mark, she would get better tips if she turned on the charm. The problem was, turning on the charm got her a little too much attention. Phone numbers slipped to her, casual touches as she refilled drinks, pickup lines that could make a stripper blush.

No. The single life was much better. She'd never been in better shape physically, and she'd never been happier emotionally. Dating random guys each week had been fun in her early twenties, but she'd grown tired of it lately, and she had decided to take a break from it all. She'd even started wearing a fake wedding ring to work, until Mark told her to take it off. "The guys want to flirt with a cute *single* waitress, Fin."

So Finley had tossed it.

"What are you waiting for?" Mark asked, scratching at his sideburns. He was probably the only man she knew who seemed to think that sideburns were somehow attractive. "You know baseball players always tip well. You've just gotta give them what they want."

Finley scowled at Mark, keeping all her retorts to herself.

Two hours, and she'd be in the boxing ring. She'd punch Star and pretend it was Mark's face. Not that Mark was exactly a bad guy, but it would feel good all the same.

Finley put on a pleasantly bland expression, loaded up her tray with six glasses of ice water, and headed over to the players.

"Welcome to the Green Falcon Pub," she cut into their bantering, speaking over the thumping music. They must have won, because they all seemed to be in a celebratory mood. Well, except for the leather jacket guy. He wasn't participating in the conversation, but stayed focused on his phone.

She proceeded to set down the water glasses. "What can I get you gentlemen to drink?"

"What do you recommend?" one of the guys asked.

She glanced over at him. His white-blond hair showed beneath his cap, and his eyes were a startling blue. His smile was friendly and easy, and she liked that. Handsome guy, but not too distracting.

"I mean, what's the Green Falcon famous for?" he continued. "We're from Baltimore, so we're looking for something memorable."

"Baltimore, huh?" she said, resting a hand on her hip. "Hmm. In that case I can recommend a couple of things." She listed the specialty beers with a smile, recommending the ones that were her favorite. Okay, so maybe she was being a little bit flirty. She never complained about getting good tips.

The guys were jovial, friendly, and not annoying after all. When it came time to ask the leather jacket guy his drink order, the blond guy elbowed him.

"What do you want, Steal? The lady's waiting."

Steal? What kind of name was that?

Leather Jacket Guy, a.k.a. Steal, raised his gaze. Finley

suddenly regretted agreeing to serve this group. Steal's eyes were a dark, murky color. Black, gray? Green? In the dim lighting of the pub, it was hard to tell exactly. And he was gazing at her like he wanted to be anyplace but in this pub. Finley tried not to take it personally, because she didn't know this guy at all, so how in the world could he be mad about *her* asking him what he wanted to drink?

His blond friend snapped his fingers, as if telling Leather Jacket Guy to speak up. "She's pretty, but we're all able to talk fine around her."

The other guys laughed. Steal's gaze didn't flinch or shift. And . . . she waited.

"Is that you on the poster?" he said, his voice low, barely audible over the thumping music of the pub.

Finley's breath stalled. She knew exactly which poster he was talking about. Mark had plastered the thing on the front door, and then back by the bathrooms. *Women's Boxing Match Saturday Night. Cover Charge $30. Fin vs. Star.* Mark had added pictures of Finley and Star. Finley's had been rather pixelated, so not too many customers put two and two together. Star's picture showed her in an exercise bra, glittery shorts, and one of her eyes painted with a giant star.

Men's sports got plenty of attention, even amateur sports. Women's sports were always a harder draw. Professional or amateur. Any exposure helped. So Finley didn't mind that Leather Jacket Guy had seen the poster. The more patrons who showed up and paid, the more Mark would be convinced to keep hosting the women's boxing events.

"It is," she said. The men around the table had quieted, and everyone seemed to have zeroed in on their conversation. Finley felt her neck heat—not at the attention—but at the way Steal's eyes had moved from her face, down the length of her body, then back up.

"Is Fin your real name?" he asked.

She wanted to lean forward to hear him better, but she remained upright. "It's short for Finley."

He gave the slightest nod, then said, "I'll have the dark imported."

It took her a second to realize he'd given her his drink order. "Oh, right, uh, I'll be back in a few with your drinks and to take your order." She'd spoken to the group at large, but her gaze continued to stray to Leather Jacket Guy.

He'd set his phone on the table, and she could see the flash of texts scrolling across the screen. But he leaned back in his chair, arms folded, his eyes only on her as if he were trying to read her mind. Or maybe size her up? Was he a boxing agent?

Her heart skipped a beat at the thought of a real sports agent watching one of her boxing matches. There were leagues much bigger than the one she was in, ones that paid more than $500 a win.

Finley would have to commit to more training, maybe even go part-time at the pub, but she was willing to do it.

Or. Leather Jacket Guy was probably a friend of one of the baseball players.

She turned away and headed toward the bar. When she reached it, she put in the drink order, then she picked up the platters of roast beef sliders, fried cheese curds, and a second round of drinks for a table of three women. She crossed to their table, deliberately stopping herself from glancing over at the baseball players again. "Here you are, ladies," she said, setting the food down.

One of the women, probably about forty, wearing cherry-red lipstick that matched her shirt, said, "Hey, can you tell Levi Cox that his next drink is on me?"

Kissing on Third

Finley hated this part of her job. Sure, pubs and bars were pickup scenes, but did they *always* have to be pickup scenes?

She glanced over at the table of baseball players. "Sure, which one is Levi Cox?"

The woman gave her a strange look. "Well, he's the one without the Blue Jays cap, because, you know, he plays for the Minnesota Ice."

Finley had no trouble picking out the guy without the hat—Leather Jacket Guy—or Steal. "I thought his name was Steal."

The woman smiled. "Oh, yeah, they call him Steal because he holds the MLB record in stealing bases."

Oh. "Can I tell him who sent him a drink?" Finley said, her throat feeling tight. She should have turned down the table of six guys. Now she'd be in the middle of a flirting ring.

"Tell him my name is Bitty." She lifted her brows, which were definitely enhanced.

"Bitty?" No way was that this woman's name.

Bitty's two friends laughed.

Whatever. "Okay, I'll give him the message."

Finley walked away and found Jess. "I'll give you all my tips tonight if you take the table of baseball guys."

"Mark says I'm hosting tonight."

"I'll give you my tips tomorrow too."

"What's this?" Mark said, coming up behind Finley.

How did he do that? Appear out of nowhere?

Busted. "Nothing," Finley said. "I'm just checking on something." She moved quickly away, hoping that Jess would keep her mouth shut. Mark didn't like waitresses leaving or switching when serving a table. Might as well get her section served. She collected the drink orders for the baseball guys, then carried them to the table.

She set down the bottles and glasses, and when she

reached Levi Cox, a.k.a. Steal, she said, "Your drink is complimentary from the table of ladies over there, sir." She tilted her head in the direction of the table. "Specifically *Bitty*, the woman in the red shirt."

The blond guy next to Levi Cox chuckled. "Nice going, Steal. You're in here for less than ten minutes, don't even look up from your phone, but already you have women buying you drinks."

Levi Cox didn't say anything for a second, and Finley wondered if that was his mojo or something. Leave everyone in suspense while he took his own sweet time to reply.

Instead of saying the usual thank you or giving Finley a message to take to the table, he pushed back his chair and stood. Finley couldn't help but follow his movements, and well, he was tall. Six foot three. Maybe taller. Even with her heels, he towered over her. He moved past her, and she barely got out of his way. A hush had fallen over the table of baseball guys as everyone seemed to be as curious as she was.

Together they watched Levi Cox walk over to the table of the three forty-something-year-old ladies. He talked to the ladies for a couple of minutes, and Finley watched in fascination as all three women blushed and smiled and laughed.

Levi Cox didn't even crack a smile as he spoke.

Then before Finley knew it, he was on the way back to the table. She stood aside, unsure what had just happened. But Levi didn't take his seat again. Instead, he reached inside his leather jacket and pulled out a wallet that had seen better days. He pulled out three hundred-dollar bills and dropped them on the table. "Enjoy your meal, boys. I'm calling it a night."

The blond guy stood. "Come on, Steal. Your presence is part of the bet, man."

"Bet's been called off," Levi said.

He cut a glance at Finley. She was now close enough to

see that his eyes were not gray or black, but a dark green. Like the color of a winter pine tree.

"Steal," his friend tried again.

But Levi Cox merely nodded to the other players. Then he walked out of the pub.

Just like that. He was gone.

"That guy's a headcase," one of the Blue Jays said.

The blond friend sat back down. "Well, that headcase is my friend, so shut up."

"Ooooh," a couple of the other players said.

"Have you guys had a chance to decide what you'd like to eat tonight?" Finley said, trying to ignore her curiosity of what Levi Cox had said to the ladies and why he'd left his table full of friends. She hadn't missed the sight of the $300 cash he'd laid down on the table like it was no big deal.

"Sorry about that," the blond guy said. "And if any of these idiots give you a hard time, they'll answer to me."

"Whatever, Rabbit," one of the Blue Jays said. "You're all about the ladies."

Rabbit? That had to be a nickname. Finley's head spun with all these names and nicknames.

Rabbit shoved his teammate's shoulder, and everyone laughed. Finley kept the smile on her face, although her thoughts had long since fled. "Must have been some bet."

"Oh, it was," Rabbit said with a wide smile. Apparently he wasn't going to expound. "I'll have the blue-cheese double-stack burger."

CHAPTER 3

"YOU'RE GOING ON a *date*?" Levi asked his brother over the phone. He'd just walked into his apartment and called Rhett to put a plan together for the weekend.

"Yeah," Rhett said with a laugh. "You know, when a guy takes a girl out to dinner, and—"

"I know what a date is, Rhett," Levi cut in. He sat on the folding chair in his living room. It was no couch, but at least the chair was padded. "I didn't know you liked someone."

"Erin's a friend," he said.

The smile was evident in his voice. Levi leaned forward and rested an elbow on his knee. "Sounds like more than a friend."

"Well, maybe she will be by the end of tomorrow night," Rhett continued. "So don't worry about coming out this weekend. You're going to cramp my style."

Levi frowned. "You have style?"

"All right, bro," Rhett said. "I'm going to go now. Need to take a test in the morning, then get a haircut."

Levi scrubbed a hand over his hair, knowing he was past due for a haircut himself. Some guys in the league grew their hair out, but Levi didn't like the upkeep. One thing was certain: if Rhett was cutting his hair, it meant something.

"Girls can be a distraction, kid," Levi said. "A big distraction."

"You've told me like four hundred times," Rhett said. "Erin's different. We study a lot together, and she's not high maintenance."

Levi blew out a breath. His brother was twenty-two, definitely old enough to get in trouble with a woman. But what should Levi say that he hadn't already over the years? "Be careful, man. Be safe. And uh, be smart."

Rhett laughed. "Thanks, bro. Have a good weekend."

"Wait," Levi said. "That's it? Have a good weekend?"

"Yeah," Rhett said. "Go do something unplanned, Levi. Mix and mingle. Maybe you should ask someone on a date. I saw that you played the Blue Jays tonight. Go hang out with Rabbit."

"We had dinner earlier," Levi said. It was only a small white lie, since they hadn't technically gotten to the eating part before the table of three women had sent over that beer. Levi might have acted rashly in some people's eyes, but he'd been through the scenario more times than he could count. A woman sent over a drink, then five minutes later, a friend would come and talk to him, then five more minutes later, the woman herself would come over. He'd feel obligated to invite her to sit down, in which case she'd drill him about baseball, money, whether he was dating, if he was looking for a fun night . . .

It was better to nip it in the bud before any of that progression happened.

"It's like ten thirty, old man," Rhett said. "You know there's a whole other world out there that happens after the elderly and small children go to bed."

Levi didn't like this conversation. "Have you been doing all your homework?"

Rhett scoffed. "This conversation is done. I'll talk to you *after* the weekend."

Before Levi could respond or even apologize, Rhett had hung up on him. Rhett was a good kid, smart, responsible, and he didn't seem to have the anger that most kids who'd been bullied had. There was no drive to fight against the norm in Rhett. Once he'd passed the awkward teenage years and hit college, he'd made fast friends. And apparently, friends with the ladies too.

Levi should be happy for his brother. But in truth, Levi was still angry about what Rhett had endured as a kid. Levi regretted his own actions too. He should have done more, protected Rhett more, stayed out of the principal's office, got in fewer fights, or no fights at all.

Levi leaned back in the folding chair and rested his head against the wall behind him. Closing his eyes, he pushed away past memories. The game had been good tonight, until things took a turn for the worse in the bottom of the fifth. Rabbit had stolen second base, and the next player up to bat hit a homer. Suddenly the game was tied up, but the morale of the Ice had plunged.

The Blue Jays had pulled out a win by one point, and thus the excursion to the Green Falcon Pub. Where a woman named Finley worked and apparently boxed too. Levi had seen plenty of boxing matches, but he had never paid much attention to the female side of the sport. And it seemed the boxing match was in the basement of the pub. At midnight.

Maybe he should go.

As soon as the thought entered his mind, he scoffed. He'd just gotten back to his apartment, and he planned to do his nightly workout, then hit the shower and bed. Without traveling tomorrow, he might catch up on some things he'd been putting off, like buying groceries for his apartment. Normally he went to the grocery store early in the morning or a half hour before closing. Fewer people that way, and fewer conversations he'd have to entertain.

Levi also switched grocery stores often, which meant a lot more driving time.

Against his will, his mind strayed to the waitress at the pub again. Her wavy, black hair had been pulled back into a ponytail, but he was sure it would reach her waist if she'd worn it down. He wasn't exactly sure what color Finley's eyes were. The pub's lighting had been dim, but he guessed them to be brown. With a lot of spark. He'd felt it the second she'd walked over to their table, although he took his sweet time looking up at her. He couldn't remember an occasion when he'd felt an instant attraction to a woman beyond an obvious acknowledgment that a woman was pretty.

With Finley ... Well, he couldn't quite explain it. But he'd known she was the woman on the boxing poster. And it had intrigued him. She couldn't weigh more than 120 pounds, 130 tops. The female boxers he'd seen were as ripped as men, complete with thick necks and corded muscles on their legs and arms.

From what Levi had seen of Finley, she was more slender than he'd have pegged for a boxer. And what did she do with all that hair when she boxed?

Levi stood. Maybe he could watch the boxing match from the back of the room. Be in and out. Not even stay for the entire match, just the first round. Then his curiosity would be sated. He'd see Finley fight, and maybe he'd figure out why she had so much fire in her eyes.

By the time Levi parked in the back lot of the pub, it was 11:45 p.m. He doubted that Rabbit and his teammates were still around, which was a good thing in Levi's opinion. He didn't want to answer their questions, because, well, he didn't know the answers himself.

Sure enough, when Levi walked into the pub, the table where he'd sat with Rabbit was filled with another party. The three ladies at the nearby table were also gone.

The hostess, with her plunging neckline, grinned up at him. "Can I get you a table?"

"Uh, where's the boxing match?"

Her blue eyes rounded. "Follow the green arrows to the basement." She pointed a bright-pink nail to her right.

"Thanks," Levi said, then moved past her before she could ask anything more. Heads turned as he walked through the pub, and he was glad no one approached him with a request for an autograph.

Once he reached the stairway leading to the underbelly of the place, he found there was a line on the stairs. The man in front of him was flushed in the face like he'd run a couple of miles to get to the pub. "You okay, man?" Levi asked.

"Yeah." The man took a gulp of air. "I thought it was at another pub, so I had to run to get here."

Levi tried not to smile. "Glad you made it."

"You look familiar . . ."

Here it was. And there was no use delaying. "I'm Levi Cox. Play for the Minnesota Ice."

The man's brows drew together. "No, that's not it. I don't follow baseball. Sorry." He shrugged. "Oh well. Maybe I'll figure it out later. I'm Patrick Dunn."

"Nice to meet you, Patrick," Levi said, wanting to laugh. But he didn't. "Do you come to these a lot?"

Patrick put his hand over his heart. "Every one. I always bet on Star. She's amazing."

"Star?" Levi said. "Is that her real name?"

Patrick cleared his throat, then looked around them, and lowered his voice. "Well, I know her real name, but I'm sworn to secrecy."

Levi nodded. "I'll honor that. What do you think of her opponent? Fin?"

Patrick rolled his eyes. "A greenie if there ever was one. Only been fighting in this league for a year. Don't know why she's matched up against Star again. The last match, Fin went down in the first round. Waste of everyone's money, if you ask me."

"Yet you're here again."

Patrick grinned. "Because of Star. I can't stay away."

Levi smiled. The man was whipped. "You, uh, friends outside of the ring?"

"Oh, nothing like that," Patrick said, his face reddening again. "She does know my name, and she has said hi to me twice, you know."

"Twice, huh?" Levi nodded. "That's great."

Patrick narrowed his eyes. "I'll bet being a baseball player gets you some attention from the ladies, right?"

"Yeah," Levi said. "But it's not always welcome, if you know what I mean."

Patrick chuckled, although his gaze looked confused. "Sure, sure. Well, you're in for a treat tonight. Got my bets placed on Star. Should walk out of here with a hundred-dollar profit."

"A hundred bucks?" Levi asked. "What's the normal betting rate these days on women's boxing?"

"Twenty, thirty," Patrick said. "I go a bit bigger myself. Fifty for Star. Worth every dollar, even if she loses once in a while."

They'd reached the bottom of the stairs, where a table was set up, taking the entrance fee. Levi handed over a hundred-dollar bill and wrote his name down on the betting list. "One please, and put the rest on Fin."

Patrick's eyes about popped out. "Fin? You crazy? She hasn't ever beat Star."

"Maybe tonight's her lucky night."

"Suit yourself, man," Patrick said. "Well, I'll see you later. Got to get to my regular place."

The man disappeared into the crowd, and Levi was left to look around the room.

The area was bigger than he thought, and next to the far wall a boxing ring had been set up. Dozens of people crowded around it, drinks in hand. Rap music played, competing with the conversation. He walked to the drink table and paid for a drink.

Ratty couches and oversized chairs lined the walls, and a few people had settled into them. But mostly everyone was gathered around the ring. Levi found a place by the wall, where he could lean against it and take in the entire room at the same time. He was surprised to see that not all those in the crowd were millennials. There were quite a few gray hairs. Maybe grandparents of the boxers? Levi had no idea.

He smiled to himself when he caught sight of Patrick gesturing wildly as he spoke to some other guy—maybe they were arguing about stats or the chances of the boxers.

Then a guy hopped up onto the ring, and Levi recognized him from the pub.

"Hey everyone!" he said into the cordless microphone. "Welcome to the match!"

Everyone yelled and cheered.

"Tonight we're excited to host our returning champion, Star!"

More yells and a few whistles. Undoubtedly from Patrick.

"And our very own Fin is here tonight, ready to take on the champ!"

The cheers were definitely more subdued, but the enthusiasm still reverberated throughout the room.

It was kind of nice to have the attention up on the boxing ring. Levi had a few glances tossed his way, but no one approached him.

"And now . . . we'd like to introduce Star!" the announcer said.

Everyone cheered as a young woman came out of a door behind the ring. She hopped up onto the ring and slipped out of a blue robe. Her face was painted in a rainbow of colors, and black outlined one of her eyes in the shape of a star. Her hair was short, spikey, and multicolor with shades of blond and blue. She must have smeared glitter on her shoulders and arms, because they sparkled in the light.

Star strutted around the ring, blowing kisses to the people calling out to her. She was built like an ox, and Levi wondered if they had some sort of weight limit, because from his point of view, Fin was going to go out in the first round again. As Star turned to face the other side of the ring, Levi caught a view of her profile. She'd definitely had her nose broken more than once. He winced. This woman was no lightweight.

"And now . . ." the announcer said. "Let's give a big welcome to the woman who's come to challenge our defending champion. Fin!"

The crowd cheered as Finley came out of the back door.

She stepped into the ring wearing a crimson robe, the red color complementing her olive skin. Her wavy, black hair was twisted into a long braid, answering his question of how she boxed with such long hair. She shrugged out of her robe.

Levi swallowed.

Maybe she wasn't built like Star, but Finley was plenty strong. The glitter on her arms and chest and stomach accented her lean muscles. She wasn't lacking any curves either, and Levi found her looking rather sexy in her red athletic spandex shorts and a sports bra. So . . . the waitressing outfit had covered up quite a bit.

Levi finished off his drink, then straightened from the wall. Maybe he would move a little closer to the ring to get a better view.

CHAPTER 4

FINLEY ROTATED HER neck and shook out her arms as the crowd outside the ring cheered their welcome. The cheers were a boost, but she knew Star was the favorite. Regardless, Finley was ready, and she had a good feeling tonight. She'd spent the last twenty minutes doing yoga stretches, and she was as limber as she was going to get.

She scanned the crowd, nodding at a couple of familiar faces. She didn't have much of a following, but there were a few regulars who came and cheered her on.

As Mark listed her fighting accolades, Finley looked toward the back of the room, where a tall guy wearing a leather jacket was leaning against the wall, drink in hand. It took her only a half second to realize that he was Levi Cox.

And he was staring right at her. She cut her gaze away and tried to focus on what Mark was saying as he reviewed the rules for the crowd. As if against her will, Finley looked at Levi again. He was still watching her. If Finley weren't nervous enough about fighting Star before, now with Levi Cox in the room, Finley's pulse skyrocketed.

She exhaled slowly, stretched her neck again, shook out

her arms. She had to focus. Not think about who might or might not be watching the fight.

Mark announced her fighting accolades, which were minimal, but Mark was somehow able to make them seem larger than they really were. Finley raised one of her boxing gloves in acknowledgment as people clapped.

Next, he listed Star's accolades, which were impressive.

The crowd was definitely favoring Star, but Fin had expected that, even in the basement of her own place of work.

The ref stepped forward and reviewed the rules to Finley and Star.

Finley barely paid attention. She knew the rules inside and out, but she should still be listening. Levi Cox had moved away from the wall and was walking toward the ring.

Breathe. In. Out. She rotated her shoulders and jogged in place. Just because Levi Cox had left the pub earlier and was now back to watch the fight, that meant nothing. Nothing personal. Maybe he liked boxing. And he would have come whether or not they'd talked.

"Do you both understand the rules?" the ref asked.

Both Finley and Star nodded their agreement. Finley refocused her gaze on Star, not blinking, not looking away. Star narrowed her blue eyes and stared back.

The ref stepped out of the middle, and Mark rang the huge cow bell he reserved for such purposes.

Finley stepped to the right the same time Star moved left. One of Star's signature moves was to strike first, and to strike fast. But Finley was ready. She ducked, then lunged forward to cuff Star in the side.

"Umph," Star said, but she didn't seem surprised or bothered. She swung again.

Finley again ducked. She could probably dodge Star's swings all night, but that was no way to win.

The crowd was shouting, or cheering—it was hard to tell. Finley moved back a step, bringing both boxing gloves in front of her face. This time she wouldn't duck, because then she could be in position to counter-swing.

Star's next swing came from the other side, and Finley blocked it, then drove her glove into the side of Star's face.

The impact was hard enough that Star reeled back. Finley knew she'd surprised Star, but Finley couldn't relax for even a second. She lunged forward and swung again. This time Star's head snapped to the side, and Finley knew that contact with her nose had been made.

Blood seeped from Star's nose, and the cow bell clanged.

Round one was over, and Star stalked to her corner to have her trainer stop the bleeding. Finley moved to her corner and tugged off a glove to use a towel over her face. She didn't have a trainer to do the honors. She'd barely been hit, but that luck wouldn't last long. Finley knew Star would be more than ready in round two.

The cow bell clanged again, and round two started.

Again, Star swung first. Finley ducked.

By round three, Finley had been hit in the jaw once, and the torso multiple times. Her torso and shoulders ached. She knew there was jaw pain, but her adrenaline ran too high to slow her down.

Round four started off more sluggish than the previous ones, and Finley swung first after circling for nearly thirty seconds. Star's focus was different this round, more feral. Finley swallowed down the smallest bit of triumph, knowing that she'd surprised the other boxer.

Star swung, and instead of ducking, Finley stepped into the swing and delivered another uppercut to Star's jaw. Star grunted but didn't lose her footing. She swung high, catching

Finley's lip, then right on top of that, Star caught Finley in the side with a hard blow.

Finley went down, gasping for air. Her vision went blurry, and she tried to roll onto her side to stand. The crowd was counting down, but Finley still couldn't catch her breath.

The ref was counting down, and then the cow bell rang, and everyone cheered.

Finley had lost.

She closed her eyes, tasting blood in her mouth.

Someone grabbed her shoulder and said something, but the sounds were all muted.

Finley dragged her eyes open, then groaned as she used her gloves to push herself up into a sitting position.

Star reached out a hand and pulled her to her feet.

Then Star released her and circled the ring, accepting all the cheers and praises.

Finley staggered back to her corner and tore off her gloves. She grabbed her water bottle and guzzled it down, wincing as it touched her mouth. She hoped she wouldn't need stitches. With the crowd still cheering for Star, Finley made her way to the back door, her mind reeling both with pain and disappointment. Five hundred bucks lost. Just like that.

She couldn't figure out how she'd gotten the breath knocked out of her. She'd endured harder hits. Finley made her way to the bathroom and surveyed the damage beneath the fluorescent light. Her lip was bleeding, but she wouldn't need stitches. Her shoulder had a pretty good bruise already starting. Looking down at her torso, she saw more marks. She'd be tender for a few days, but nothing she hadn't been through before.

Mostly she was disappointed in herself.

"You did good, kid," Mark said.

Finley turned see him leaning against the doorframe.

"Four rounds against Star," he said. "Major improvement." His voice bounced off the walls, hurting her head.

"Thanks," she said, her voice dull. But she couldn't muster any more enthusiasm.

"Do you need anything?" Mark asked.

"I'm good," she said. Mark was a decent boss, but she didn't like it when he got in her personal space.

He scratched at one of his sideburns. "Do you need me to drive you home?"

"No, I'm walking." She lived only a couple of blocks away. The night air would clear her head. Then she'd get to her apartment, soak in an ice bath, take some aspirin, and go to bed.

"Okay, then," Mark said. "Did you know that Levi Cox bet seventy dollars on you?"

Finley didn't move, didn't respond.

"He gave the cashier a hundred-dollar bill. I think a seventy-dollar bet is your record," Mark said with a chuckle. "Nice job, kid."

She shrugged, then turned on the faucet, hoping that would give Mark the hint to leave. She splashed water on her face, and when she next looked up, he was gone.

The sounds of celebrating still came from the other room, then Star's voice sounded on the microphone. Well, it was her night. Time for Finley to go home.

She pulled on some yoga pants and a T-shirt, then grabbed her duffle bag. She headed out the back door and up the stairs that led to the parking lot behind the pub.

The parking lot was full, but would empty out soon enough. As she passed beneath a street lamp, she saw a motion from the corner of her eye. Her heart skipped a beat, and she looked over to see a guy leaning against an old Bronco. He was silhouetted in the shadows, but his height reminded her of Levi Cox.

"Hey," he said in a quiet voice, hands in his pockets, not moving from his position.

Finley stopped. Definitely Levi Cox. She exhaled. "Hey."

"You, uh, okay?" he asked.

She could feel his eyes on her, and it sent warm shivers across her skin. Or maybe it was because of the night's breeze brushing past her.

"Yeah," she said. "Just a little bruised."

He nodded.

"That your Bronco?"

He straightened then, stepped away from the truck, then looked at it as if he were trying to decide. "Yeah. I bought it in college. Haven't been able to get rid of her."

"*Her?*" Finley walked toward the Bronco, keeping her gaze on the truck while feeling Levi's gaze on her.

"She's temperamental," he said in a low voice.

"So you dubbed it a *she*."

His smile was faint, but it was there.

And Finley's heart thumped in response. She kept walking until she reached the front of the Bronco. Whatever year it was, it was in immaculate shape. "I thought you'd have a sports car, like a Porsche at the very least."

"I don't think I could fit into a Porsche."

For some reason, his comment made her face warm. She glanced over at him. "What about a Ferrari?"

His eyes were dark, unreadable. "My former teammate has one, but it's not really my style."

Finley felt her lips twitch, but she held back a smile. "Still . . . you're a pro baseball player." She ran her hand over the hood and walked toward the side he stood on. "You know, throwing around hundred-dollar bills like they're quarters."

He took a step closer, hands still in his pockets. "When I was a kid, my foster dad brought home a hundred-dollar bill one night. He showed it to me and my brother. Told us that if we worked hard enough then one day we could have our own hundred-dollar bill. It seemed impossible at the time, but when I got my first paycheck from the league, I cashed it into all hundred-dollar bills."

Finley leaned against the Bronco and folded her arms. "And you started dropping them on the tables at pubs?"

"I'd rather pay cash when I'm out in public," he said, leaning against the truck as well. "Too many stories of stolen credit cards."

Finley looked over at him, raising her brows. They were several feet apart, but she was aware of everything about him. The angle of his jaw, the depths of his eyes, the broad set of his shoulders, and his long, lean build.

He met her gaze, not shying away from looking at her. Which only made her feel warm again.

"And it's easier to make a quick getaway from all those women's phone numbers coming your way?" she said.

"You caught me."

Finley smiled, then blew a hiss through her teeth. She touched her swollen bottom lip. "Don't make me smile."

He moved closer and leaned down. "You need to get some ice on that," he said. "A black tea bag helps with swelling too."

She lowered her hand. "A tea bag? Never heard of that." He hadn't moved away, and she caught the scent of leather and something like spice and pine.

"You steep it for a few minutes," he said, "then put the tea bag on the swollen area."

"Sounds like you have some experience," she said.

"The wrong kind of experience."

"Okay, maybe I'll try it." She pushed away from the Bronco because Levi was standing rather close, and she was feeling too warm. She should really be soaking in that ice bath about now. "I need to go. The aspirin's calling my name. Thanks for coming to the match, uh, Levi, or Steal, or whatever your name is."

The edge of his mouth lifted. "Levi's fine."

"Well, then, Levi, have a good night." She stepped back, then back again. Turning, she started across the parking lot.

"You're walking?" he asked.

He hadn't spoken very loudly, but with no one else around, his words were clear. She looked over her shoulder. "I don't live far."

"There's nothing wrong with the Bronco," he said. "I could give you a ride, if you're not opposed to a car that's not a Porsche."

She stopped and turned to face him. "I'm sure your truck is perfectly fine. I . . . don't really know you, Levi Cox, even though you blew a hundred bucks on my boxing match tonight. So I'm walking home, like I already planned."

He walked toward her, and she could only watch him. What was he doing?

When he neared, he stopped. "How about we compromise? I walk you home. Then I come back here and drive my Bronco to my place."

"I'm seriously fine," she said. "I really don't expect—"

"Look, it's the middle of the night," he cut in. "This neighborhood isn't exactly Mayberry."

"I *am* a boxer," she said.

He smiled. Really smiled. More than just Finley's face went hot.

"I know," he said, still smiling. "But I'd still like to walk you home. If that's all right with you."

Chapter 5

Yep. There was still fire in Finley's eyes, Levi decided, even though she'd lost her match tonight. He'd expected to see more bruising on her face, but only her lip was swollen. She moved a bit carefully, and he imagined she was pretty sore. Her yoga pants and blue T-shirt covered up that red number she'd worn in the boxing ring, and he should probably stop thinking about what she may or may not be wearing under her clothing.

He fully expected her to turn him down flat when he offered to walk her home. But to his surprise, she said, "Okay then. Come on. I'm about ready to drop dead anyway, so I probably wouldn't be able to fight off any bad guys."

"I have a perfectly nice Bronco about twenty steps away," Levi said.

She started walking toward the street. So . . . no Bronco.

Levi followed, catching up easily. He wasn't really sure he wanted to analyze why he was walking this woman home in the middle of the night after her boxing match. He'd only met her a couple of hours ago, and he knew almost nothing about her. If Rabbit knew what Levi was doing, he'd catch all kinds of crap. Or Rhett.

But Levi was curious.

"Finley's a unique name," he said, glancing over at her. She walked with the slightest limp. "Are you named after someone?" Here he went with the questions. They sort of tumbled out.

"Yeah, well, my dad used to play college football in Tennessee," she said, her gaze connecting with his, then shifting away. "Named me after the stadium. Lucky me."

"Is that where you're from?" he asked.

She cut him a glance. "I was born in Tennessee, but I didn't live there long. After my mom left, my dad moved us to his parents' in Minnesota. Been here ever since."

"I guess that's one reason to live in Minnesota. Family. Because the weather sure isn't much of a draw."

Finley laughed, then she shoved his arm. "I told you not to make me laugh."

"Sorry." He wasn't sorry. When she smiled or laughed, her dimples appeared. "And Fin, is that a stage name, or your nickname?"

"It's what Mark calls me, and what he put on the poster." She shrugged, then winced. She rubbed her neck.

"Who's Mark?" So many questions. Levi wanted to laugh at himself.

"My boss at the pub, and the guy who did the announcing," she said. "He's been a big supporter of women's boxing."

She folded her arms, and he could swear she shivered. The warm, humid night was far from cold. "Are you cold?"

"No," she said. "I shiver after matches. A reaction from my body, I guess."

Levi shrugged off his jacket.

"I'm fine, really," she protested.

But when he set the jacket around her shoulders, she slipped her arms into the sleeves.

"Your body's cooling off after so much heat," he said.

Finley nodded.

Levi decided that she looked really good in his leather jacket. The dark color made her eyes almost black.

"So . . . where did you grow up?" she asked.

"Florida."

She scoffed. "Say no more. I can picture your childhood in my mind. Twenty-four seven sun and blue skies. Spending weekends at the beach with your family."

"Foster family."

"Whatever." Finley pulled the jacket close to her body. "Winters were balmy. Driving with the top down on your convertible in the middle of December."

"I didn't have a car."

"Your foster dad's car, then." She smirked. "You driving, your girlfriend in the seat next to you as the warm sea breeze flows through her long blond hair."

"No girlfriend either," he said. "Changed schools a lot."

"Then your little brother and his girlfriend. She had long blond hair."

Levi laughed. "You have a good imagination."

"Keeps us Minnesotans sane in the dregs of winter." She spread her arms. "But you can't complain tonight. The weather is pretty much perfect. Seventy-five degrees, moderate humidity."

"I'm not complaining tonight," he said. He also couldn't stop looking at her.

She smiled over at him.

He smiled back.

"So . . . Mr. Florida," she said, slowing to a stop and turning to face him. "You play baseball. Have a little brother. Know how to treat swelling on facial wounds. Always pay in cash. Anything else I should know?"

He gazed down at her. "What do you want to know?"

Her lips curved. "Why are you here?"

"Like *right here*? On this sidewalk?"

"Yeah."

"Just walking a pretty woman home."

"I told you not to make me laugh," she said, her cheeks dimpling. "I don't need a mirror to tell me what I look like tonight."

Was she asking for more compliments by turning down the first one? Because he could dish them out. "I don't mind a little sweat."

She did laugh then. "Well, thanks for making me feel like I wasn't a complete failure tonight."

"From what I heard, you exceeded everyone's expectations."

She wrinkled her nose, then touched her fingers to her swollen lip. "I thought I was ready for her. I guess I was cocky a little too soon."

"Where do you train?" Levi asked.

She looked past him, at the building behind them. "Right there."

He glanced over his shoulder. "Is that a gym?" The place looked like an apartment building, but maybe there was a gym inside.

"No, my apartment," she said. "I have some weights and an ancient treadmill."

Levi frowned. "You don't go to a gym?"

She shrugged. "I sort of like to do things my own way, you know, and not with a bunch of people watching me. Or Muscle Mikes trying to get my number."

"Muscle Mikes?"

She seemed to hesitate. "Those guys with necks thicker

than their arms, who use the gym as a place to pick up women."

"That bad, huh?"

She didn't answer his question. "Well, thanks for walking me. I'll let you return to your regularly scheduled night before . . . all of this."

So she was calling it a night, just like that. Not that he could blame her. She needed ice and aspirin and recovery time.

"See you later, Mr. Florida," she said, moving past him.

He watched her walk up the steps to the building. "Bye, Finley." He didn't even know her last name. And it occurred to him after she'd disappeared into the building that she was still wearing his jacket. He hadn't gotten her number or anything, but at least he knew where to find her.

His cell phone buzzed with a text, and Levi pulled his phone out of his pocket. The Six Pack group text was in full swing. Levi must have been in a dead area, because his phone had been silent when he was with Finley. Now he saw that he'd missed over a dozen texts. Congratulations to Rabbit on the win, tongue-in-cheek consolations to Levi, followed by a shout-out to Axel, a.k.a. Axe Man, for another homerun tonight in Seattle for the Sharks. The guy was on fire.

Sawyer Bennet, a.k.a. Skeeter, had pitched a no-hitter. And Cole Hunter—Big Dawg—had caught three flyballs in centerfield. All in all, it had been a good night. Even Grizz's team had won at home in Pittsburgh.

Then Levi grimaced. Unbeknownst to him, Rabbit had taken a picture of when Levi went to talk to the ladies at the pub. The picture showed Levi's back and two of the ladies grinning up at him. The sight made him a little sick. The admiration in their gazes was nothing more than seeing him as a professional baseball player with a lucrative paycheck.

None of those women knew anything about him besides his name.

In fact, he'd told Finley more about himself than he'd told even his Minnesota Ice teammates.

Rabbit texted: *The Ice Man breaking hearts one at a time in the Mini Apple.* Followed by a bunch of crying-face emojis.

Those women don't look cold at all, Skeeter wrote. *I thought you said Minnesota was cold.*

Levi scoffed, and wrote. *It's July. I dare you to come visit me in February.*

Can't, Skeeter replied. *I'll be in preseason.*

Then January.

Done. It's a date, Skeeter wrote. *Anyone else in?*

The phone chimed with the replies.

Levi smiled as he continued walking to the parking lot at the pub. These guys usually followed through on their threats.

Speaking of July, you all still in for Belltown Days? Rabbit wrote.

When is that? Grizz texted.

Next Friday.

Levi wrote, *I'll be there.*

Nice, Rabbit replied. *Who else?*

Scheduling my private jet right now, Big Dawg said. *Want me to pick anyone up on the way?*

Me, Grizz wrote.

I'm out. Sorry, guys, Skeeter said.

But that's your freaking hometown, Rabbit wrote.

We're playing in Arizona that night.

Are you in the pitching rotation? Rabbit asked.

Doesn't matter, Skeeter said. *I can't ditch.*

Levi was confident they'd all work it out. The Minnesota Ice had a bye next Friday, and Levi was planning on flying in Friday afternoon, then out Saturday morning back to

Minneapolis for his game. Their college coach, Rich Maxwell, would be there, of course, the guy who'd recruited him out of high school to play for the Belltown University Lumberjacks.

Levi turned off his phone and slipped it into his pocket. He had other things on his mind. Namely, how his brother's weekend would turn out. And he wondered if Finley worked at the pub tomorrow. He wasn't flying out until Sunday with his team, so he had some time on his hands.

Chapter 6

Finley stared at the patch of sunlight moving across her ceiling. She hadn't slept much the night before, and now that morning was here, there was no hope of falling back asleep. Her mind wouldn't shut off last night. It was usually like that after a fight, but she wasn't thinking of how she could have brought down Star, but how she'd come to spend part of the evening with Levi Cox. Finley had forgotten to return his jacket, which meant she had to figure out how to get it back to him.

Maybe she could look him up on Instagram or something, but she was kind of afraid to look him up. It was easier to believe last night had been one of those weird cosmic events, one that would never repeat itself. Learning more about Levi Cox, and seeing his plethora of pictures, would only make her mind obsess over him more.

Yeah. Because she was definitely obsessing.

Finley turned over in her bed and pushed herself into a sitting position. Pain lanced through her shoulder and torso. Not surprising. She needed more aspirin. As of this moment, her lip didn't hurt, but that might change when she tried to talk.

She shoved aside her blanket and walked to the bathroom, bypassing the row of chairs she had lined up in the hallway. They were dining room chairs she was refinishing, then hoped to sell at the monthly swap meet.

In the bathroom, she flipped on the light. Her hair was a tangled mess, and her face was ... Oh boy. She moved closer. She had bruising on her cheek, but not on either of her eyes. Her nose was fine too. But her bottom lip had turned purple. At least the swelling was mostly gone.

She'd borrowed some black tea bags from her neighbor last night, and they'd worked pretty well.

Finley turned her head. Very well. The swelling was barely noticeable; just the discoloring remained.

"Well, Mr. Florida, you were right," she said to her reflection. "Who would have thought?"

She stared into the mirror. Her brown eyes were dull from lack of sleep, and her T-shirt hopelessly wrinkled.

"Okay, I give up," she murmured. "I'm going to google him."

After making herself instant coffee, she climbed into her bed and pulled up the covers, then turned on her phone.

Three texts appeared on the screen. One from Jess: *I woke up super sick this morning, can you cover my shift?*

The next from Mark: *Need you to come in today to cover for Jess. Sorry. I know you're probably still sore.*

Jess again: *I think I have food poisoning.* Then she added the vomit emoji.

Nice. Finley was supposed to have the entire day off. Now she'd have to cancel lunch plans with her dad since she'd be working a double shift. She texted both Mark and Jess back. *I can be there by eleven.* The pub wouldn't start to get busy until right before the lunch hour, and Finley figured she'd earned a couple of hours of downtime this morning. It was 8:30 a.m.

She'd do her yoga routine in a bit, but that's all she allowed herself the day after a fight. Waitressing Jess's shift would be enough physical activity.

Finley settled back onto her pillows and opened the browser on her phone. She typed in: *Levi Cox Minnesota Ice*.

His bio popped up, and she scanned the details. Levi was from Florida. His younger brother's name was Rhett. Levi had played college baseball at Belltown University in Western Massachusetts. He was six foot four. Birthday July 28. So, almost twenty-seven. Amazing, the things she could find out with a single Google search. He played third base, and yep, he held the current MLB record for stealing bases. She clicked on *Images*. And there he was. All six feet, four inches of him, wearing a blue baseball uniform with black lettering.

The first picture was of him speaking to a reporter lady. Levi was clean-shaven, unlike how he'd been last night, and his eyes were ... Finley zoomed in. Then she found another picture to zoom into. *Dark green*, she decided. Next she clicked on some YouTube videos and watched him batting, catching balls, and stealing bases, some of the labeled plays of the day by various sports networks.

With each video clip, her heart rate only went up a notch.

Finley closed the browser and shut her eyes. So ... Levi Cox had watched her boxing match last night. Had waited for her in the parking lot. Had walked her home. Had given her his jacket.

She didn't know what to think. About him. About what he'd done and why.

Last night he'd been ... sweet, and kind of flirty, and well, acting *interested*. In *her*.

Finley climbed out of her bed, purposely leaving her phone on the nightstand; otherwise she'd be wasting the next two hours staring at pictures of Levi Cox. She was so not a fan girl of anyone. And Levi Cox had thousands of fans. Finley had had front-row seats to how women acted around him. *Forty-year-old* women. Twenty-year-old women would probably throw their panties in his direction.

Finley sighed and walked into her kitchen. She blended up a protein drink, adding two bananas, then settled on one of the four overstuffed chairs in the living room. She also had two couches and a loveseat in the space. She'd buy the furniture at garage sales, then reupholster them and sell them at a profit at the swap meet. Usually the refurbished furniture brought in a decent profit, which was how she could afford an apartment on her own and not have to rely on a roommate. A far-fetched dream was to refinish furniture full-time, but she didn't even have close to the money saved that she would need for something like that.

Finley drank the protein shake slowly, trying not to gag as she did. Unless she added straight-up sugar, the stuff was always a tad bitter.

Finley was determined to do whatever it took to let her body recover and to stay healthy. Since she'd lost to Star, Finley's next match was in two weeks against Shirley Temple. No, not the 1950s child actress, but a woman with the craziest curly hair. Finley had beaten her twice and had lost twice. So their match would be a draw. Although with Finley going down in the fourth round against Star, Finley was now a few points ahead of Shirley Temple in the season.

After yoga and a shower, Finley called her dad.

"Don't tell me you're canceling," he said, skipping any *Hello, how are you doing?*

"Sorry, Dad," she said. "One of the waitresses has food poisoning, and the other one is on vacation. So I'm working a double shift. Come into the pub, and I'll serve you up the special."

"How can I stay mad when you make me an offer like that?"

Finley laughed. "The offer stands any time I'm on shift. Are you coming?"

Her dad sighed. "Here's the thing. After our now-canceled lunch, I sort of made bowling plans."

"That's great," Finley said. Her dad had been part of a city league for a few years, but then had quit after a back injury at work. "Is it with the league?"

"No," he said. "A couple of the guys—you'd remember them. Chad and Brent."

"The brothers?"

"Yep."

"Well, bring them to the pub after," she said. "Those bowling alley nachos only go so far."

Her dad chuckled. "You're a good kid. Sorry about your loss last night."

"I'm over it," Finley said, and she mostly was. "I fight Shirley Temple in two weeks. Wanna come?"

"Is it at midnight again?"

"Yeah, you know that's the only time Mark can get it booked and not detract from the pub's business."

"I'll see how the Friday before goes," her dad said. "I'm no spring chicken anymore. Those midnight matches about do me in."

"You could crash at my place after so you don't have to drive home."

"Your couch hates me."

Finley laughed. Her dad had stayed over at her apartment once, and she'd heard nothing but complaints for the next three weeks. "All right, we'll talk soon. Hopefully Chad and Brent will be hungry, and I'll see you later today."

After hanging up with her dad, Finley finished getting

ready for work. Her waitress outfit was the standard black pants and white blouse. She spritzed her hair, then finger-combed it and fixed it into a loose ponytail. Then she put in small American-flag earrings. The Fourth of July was on Monday, but it was never too early to celebrate the country's independence.

She fastened a few bracelets on her wrists, a series of leather bands, woven ones, and silver chains. Next, she grabbed her shoulder bag, then picked up Levi Cox's jacket. It was too hot to wear it right now, so she folded it over her arm, figuring he might come to the pub at some point to pick it up.

Not to see her. No. For his jacket.

But a girl could hope, right?

By the time she reached the pub, Finley was plenty warm, both from the humid summer air and because thoughts of Levi Cox had invaded her mind again.

"Thanks for coming in," Mark said as soon as she stepped into the restaurant. He was manning the hostess stand.

"No problem," Finley said. Yeah, her body wanted the rest, but her bank account needed the money.

Mark scanned her face. "You look better than I thought you would. Won't be scaring the customers away after all."

Finley smirked. "A couple of beers, and no one will notice a thing."

"That a girl," Mark said with a wink. "Keep serving 'em up."

Finley passed by him and headed to the kitchen and the employee lockers. She set her bag and the leather jacket in her locker. Then she tied on a half apron. She slipped her order pad and cell phone in each of the pockets.

During the first hour of working, she turned to look at every patron who stepped into the pub, her pulse jumping each time it was a man. But Levi Cox didn't show up. Not the first hour or the hours following.

When Jess's shift was well past over, and Finley was technically into her regular shift, she stopped watching the door. She was tired, and she'd even cracked open a can of caffeinated soda, though she usually swore off the stuff. She had to keep moving, keep being cheerful to the customers, keep pulling in the tips. The Saturday crowd was always different than any other night. Customers were more relaxed, stayed longer, ordered extra drinks, tipped better.

"You holding up okay?" Mark had asked her a couple of times.

"If you don't keep reminding me how tired I should be," she finally said, "I'd forget how tired I am."

"Okay." Mark raised both hands. "No more questions of care and concern."

Normally Finley didn't mind the teasing Mark, but her head was pounding. She detoured toward the kitchen and took another swallow of her soda. She should probably eat too. "I'm taking ten," she told Jensen, one of the other waiters.

"Every table is full," he said. "And there's a thirty-minute wait."

Finley shrugged. She untied her apron and headed toward the back door, grabbing a sandwich from the employee counter where the chef would put messed-up orders. Once outside, she leaned against the pub wall. The parking lot was full. Maybe she didn't need an entire ten minutes.

As she ate, she closed her eyes, letting the cooler night air and the quiet soak into her. Her headache was in full force, and she knew that only sleep would get rid of it. Maybe working a double shift had been too much after all. Besides, she was pretty sure that Levi Cox wasn't coming tonight. It was nearly 11:00 p.m., and there hadn't been a Minnesota Ice game tonight. She'd looked up their schedule.

When she'd eaten half the sandwich, she gave up and tossed the rest into the trash. She pulled the door open and went back into the kitchen.

Jensen was in the kitchen collecting an order. "Mark's looking for you."

"Great," Finley muttered. She drank more caffeinated soda, tied her apron back on, then headed into the restaurant. She carried a water pitcher to do refills. Mark could find her. She'd been gone for only six or seven minutes.

As she left the kitchen, her steps slowed.

Mr. Florida.

Levi Cox was sitting in her section. And he was alone. Jacketless, of course. He wore a plain black T-shirt that looked anything but plain on him. Finley caught a view of the corded muscles of his arms, the broad set of his shoulders, and the fact that he'd shaved. His dark-blond hair had that mussed look as if he'd run his fingers through it more than once.

Her brain told her to keep walking, but her feet wouldn't move. He was probably with someone, or he wouldn't be ordering anything, right? It would be kind of weird to get a table for one in a crowded restaurant on a weekend night.

Move, Finley commanded herself. As she refilled the waters at a table in her section, she saw from her peripheral vision that Levi was still sitting by himself. He ignored everything around him, scrolling through his phone, and didn't seem to be looking for her. But, clearly, he'd want his jacket back.

Maybe he was waiting for someone? One of his baseball friends, or even ... another woman? Finley should hurry to the kitchen and fetch his jacket. Then he could go about his night. Or maybe ... he'd *asked* to be seated in her section?

Finley exhaled, water pitcher gripped in her hand, and turned to go find out if Levi Cox wanted to put in an order. On the way, she set the water pitcher on a side counter, then continued through the tables.

"Ma'am, can we get another order of fries?" a man said.

Finley slowed. "Certainly. I'll be back in a few minutes."

She continued toward Levi's table. He was still focused on his phone.

When she stopped at his table, she said, "Missing a jacket?"

Levi looked up.

Finley held back a sigh. Because no picture on the internet did Levi Cox justice, not compared to him in the flesh. His dark-green eyes focused on her, making her feel warmer than she should. Levi immediately scanned her face, then the rest of her, and she knew what he was looking for.

"Thanks for the tea bag idea," she said, tapping her lip. "It worked pretty well."

The edge of his mouth lifted, but he still hadn't said anything.

"My neighbor had some tea bags, so lucky for me," she continued, carrying the one-sided conversation. "And luckily she answered her door at one thirty in the morning."

He still wasn't saying anything, just studying her. She'd love to know what was going on in that head of his.

"Want me to grab your jacket now, or are you also looking to order something?" she said. "I can offer you the employee discount, since, you know, you helped me out last night. A discount for you and your . . . friend. Are you waiting for someone?"

"Just you," he said, setting his phone face down.

Something warm shivered through Finley, but she ignored it.

"And I'm alone," he continued in that low, rustic voice of his. "I didn't exactly have your number. I don't even know your last name."

"Gray." So he had come here to get his jacket, to see her, to . . .

"Well, Finley Gray, I think I will order food. What do you recommend?"

The question shouldn't have caught her off guard, but it took her a few seconds to process. "The sliders are excellent. And the berry brie salad."

One of his brows rose. "Are you sure? You seem hesitant."

"I'm sure," she said. "It's been a long day. I've been here since eleven."

Levi glanced at his phone. "That's like . . . more than twelve hours. Is that legal?"

She shrugged. "It's a double shift. Jess was sick. And Saturdays are crazy busy."

He held her gaze. "You do look tired."

"You're not supposed to say that to a woman, you know," she said. "It's not exactly complimentary; besides, I don't need to be told I look tired. I already know. It's like me pointing out that you shaved."

His mouth quirked, then he stroked his jaw. "It was a slow day." He leaned back in his chair. "Besides, me saying that you look tired isn't meant to get under your skin. I'm wondering why your boss couldn't cover your shift, especially when he's the one who knows what happened last night more than anyone."

"I'm fine," Finley said.

"You say that a lot."

Finley rested her hand on her hip. "That's because it's true."

He smiled.

Finley's heart did a somersault.

"I'll have both," he said.

"Both?"

"The sliders and the berry brie salad," he said in that maddeningly sexy voice of his.

"Okay, great." She hated that she sounded breathless. "And to drink?"

"You choose." He was still smiling.

"Really?"

"Really."

"Okay, then . . ." Apparently he wasn't going to give her a break, no matter how tired she looked. "I'll be back in a minute with your mystery drink." Then she turned and walked away before she could smile back at him.

Chapter 7

Levi watched Finley Gray walk away from his table, and he probably shouldn't be staring after her. But he was fascinated. She was even prettier than he remembered, and he had a good memory. Though she did look tired, and he was seriously considering having a word with her boss. Mark?

Levi scanned the pub for signs of the manager, but he didn't see him. The place was packed, and the conversation and chatter and music all blended together into one throbbing sound. He'd rather be someplace quieter, with Finley. So maybe he'd ask her out . . . would that be too far-fetched?

He didn't even know if she had a boyfriend. He should probably find that out first.

Levi sighed and picked up his phone. His brother hadn't texted him back all day. Was Rhett really going to stick to what he said about not talking to him until Monday? His other texts consisted of the group chat with the Six Pack. The chat had been going off the last thirty minutes as games had finished for the night.

Not hearing from Rhett and waiting for a good time to come back to the pub had made today long as hell. If Levi had known Finley was working all day, he would have come earlier. As it was, he'd figured the restaurant would slow down a bit after 11:00 p.m., but he'd been wrong. Every table was filled, with more people waiting in the lobby.

Levi scanned the place, not feeling a bit guilty about sitting alone at a table for four. He'd come to eat, like everyone else, and to get his jacket. But in reality, he would have come anyway. To see her again. And to know if his brain had just been in a weird place last night.

Finley came out of the kitchen, carrying a platter of fries and a bottle of beer. She stopped by a table to deliver the fries and smiled at something the customer said. Her dimples flashed. Levi probably shouldn't be checking her out, but he was. He'd noticed her American-flag earrings and all those bracelets that had jangled when she put her hand on her hip. Her long, dark hair was pulled into a loose ponytail, and she seemed to be wearing some sort of glittery eye makeup.

And now she was walking in his direction, her hips swaying ever so slightly and those brown eyes flashing.

He was smiling before she reached his table.

"What did you bring me?" he asked.

She set down a bottle. "Something you'll like."

He turned the bottle to read the label—one he wasn't familiar with. "How can you be sure?"

She smiled. This time at *him*. Which was much better.

"Just try it, Mr. Florida."

So he did. Took a long swallow of the smooth, cold drink. "It's good. Thanks."

"You're welcome," she said. "Be back soon with your meal."

"Wait," Levi said before she could disappear again. "What time do you get off?"

"I'm closing, so around one thirty."

"And you're walking home again?"

Finley rested her hand on her hip.

He kind of liked it when she did that.

"I'll be fine," she said.

Levi held back a smile. "I know, but I had something to ask you that's kind of personal."

This brought her brows up. "You can ask me here. I'm not worried about being overheard, with all the noise."

Levi glanced around as if he were checking to see if someone was listening. "It's *extremely* personal."

Her lips twitched. "You're really going to wait two hours to ask me something?"

"Or I could text you," he said. "You know, that would be private too."

Finley laughed. "Wow, you are *smooth*, Levi Cox. I've never been asked for my number quite like that."

He picked up his phone, waiting.

She held out her hand, and he set his phone in it. Seconds later, she'd entered her contact information, then she gave him the phone back.

Before she made it to the kitchen, he'd already sent the text: *Do you have a boyfriend?*

She disappeared into the kitchen. And he waited. And waited.

No reply.

Eventually she came back out of the kitchen, took more orders, delivered food, refilled drinks. She brought him another drink without saying a word.

When she brought him his meal, she still didn't say anything about his text.

Was she trying to kill him?

Well, he could wait it out.

Her text came when he was almost finished eating his meal.

I don't have a boyfriend. And I'm not married, and I'm not divorced, if those are your next questions.

Levi grinned. He looked up from his phone and scanned the pub for her. She must be in the kitchen again. He texted: *Can I walk you home after work? Or we can take the Bronco.*

No reply. Not that he was surprised. He finished his meal, and as he was pushing back his chair, Finley appeared. Holding his jacket.

"Bad news," she said.

He rose to his feet and looked down at her, wondering how he'd missed her approach.

"The boss says we're only taking cash tonight," she said, handing him the jacket. "Specifically in hundred-dollar bills."

She was trying not to break into a smile.

Levi took the jacket, then pulled out his wallet from his back pocket. "I guess I'm in luck then." He took out a hundred-dollar bill, then set it on the table. "Keep the change, Finley Gray."

Levi moved past her, then strode to the door. Once outside, he headed for the parking lot. He opened the door to the Bronco and tossed in the jacket. Then he pulled out his phone. She still hadn't replied to his text. But he would wait.

He spent the next hour watching YouTube videos on the Pittsburgh Knights, whom he'd be playing against tomorrow night. He rewatched plays by the second baseman and third baseman, to see how they threw and caught, searching for any weaknesses. Next, he watched videos on the catcher, David McCarthy. A.k.a. Grizz. A member of the Six Pack.

Grizz had been the first one to befriend Levi when he'd arrived in Belltown his freshman year. Somehow Grizz had read up on Levi's high school stats.

"Hey, Steal," Grizz had greeted him when Levi walked into the Belltown U team locker room.

Even then, Grizz was wearing his signature aviator glasses. Indoors. His beard wasn't as thick as it was now, since it was more artsy back then. Levi hadn't ever been big on personal appearance upkeep. Got his hair cut every couple of months. Shaved or didn't shave. That was it.

"Steal?" Levi had questioned Grizz. "I think you've got the wrong person."

"The way I see it," Grizz had said, "you averaged fifty stolen bases a season during your high school career. So we're calling you Steal."

The guy was about an inch taller than Levi, but built more like a racehorse. "And what should I call *you*, David McCarthy?"

Grizz had grinned. "Grizz."

"Nothing to do with baseball, huh?"

Grizz pulled off his aviator glasses and fixed Levi with his ice-blue eyes. "Some players don't need their baseball skills defined. Like me. It's all about the hair."

Levi had laughed then. And he soon learned that whenever things were stressful, or feeling out of control, Grizz could lighten his mood.

Now, it was one in the morning, but Levi was tempted to call Grizz. Levi wouldn't have time in the morning, between flying out to Pittsburgh and warm-ups at the Knights' field. If Grizz was asleep and hadn't turned his phone off, then that was his problem.

Grizz answered on the first ring. "You have terrible timing as usual, Steal."

It was an old joke between them. "You got a woman over?"

Grizz chuckled. "You think I would have answered a call from anyone, especially someone from the Six Pack, if I did?"

Levi smiled and leaned against the Bronco. "Good point."

"What's up, Steal?" he asked. "Wanna make a bet? Loser has to streak down Main Street after the game?"

"Ha. We're not in college anymore," Levi said. "We're grown men, remember?"

"That's what makes it all the more fun," Grizz answered, a smirk in his voice. "We're old enough to know better, yet stupid stuff happens anyway."

"No thanks," Levi said.

"So why are you calling me at one in the morning?" Grizz asked.

Levi rubbed his hand over his face, stalling.

"A woman, huh?" Grizz said. "What's going on? She's got her hooks into you?"

"I don't know what's going on," Levi said. "I haven't been in this situation before."

"Well, if you're calling me for advice, I'm going to need a little more to go on than that."

Levi pushed away from the Bronco and walked the length of the parking lot. "I've never had to work like this before. She's not like any other woman I've met."

Grizz chuckled. "You mean she's not buying you drinks?"

"Yeah, about that. Rabbit should have kept his mouth shut," Levi grumbled. "I can't believe he took a picture."

"Believe me, there's a big difference between college baseball and Major League baseball when it comes to some women," Grizz said. "We've all experienced it."

"Yeah, but I can blow that stuff off." Levi paused by the back fence, beyond which was another building. An apartment building, by the looks of it. "She's sort of hard to read."

Grizz didn't say anything for a minute. "What's her vibe?"

Levi frowned. "Her *what?*"

"You know, how do you feel around her, and how do you think she feels around *you?*"

Levi rubbed the back of his neck. "Uh, that's really deep."

Grizz laughed. "Women are deep. At least women who are worth getting to know."

Levi blew out a breath. "I think she's interested. She's sweet, you know, but tough as hell. She's a boxer."

"Whoa," Grizz said. "Hold up. A boxer? As in she'll punch your lights out if you look at her wrong?"

Levi smiled. "She's a lightweight."

"*So* much better." Grizz cleared his throat as if he were trying to hold back a laugh. "I don't know, man. A boxer chick? All that muscle, nothing soft."

"She's plenty soft," Levi said, scratching the edge of his jaw. It felt prickly. "I mean, not that I've actually *touched* her. But she's curvy, and yeah, she's strong, but not like a bodybuilder or anything." He should stop talking. Sharing these details could get him into trouble.

"Do you have a picture?" Grizz asked.

Levi scoffed. "Really? Why would you go there?"

"Easy, Steal," Grizz said. "You got me curious, that's all. Boxer or ballet dancer, I'm wondering about the woman who finally turned Levi Cox's stubborn head."

"Funny." Levi walked toward his Bronco. He had to keep moving. This conversation was about as uncomfortable as he'd ever had.

"Did you get her number?" Grizz asked.

Levi smiled. "Yeah."

"Then call her. Text her. Whatever seems right," Grizz said. "All I know is that if she's worth something to you, don't screw it up before anything can start. Which means not making assumptions, and taking things at *her* pace, not yours."

Levi nodded to himself. Made sense. "Okay. I can handle that, I think."

Grizz's chuckle was soft. "Just remember that women are not like a baseball game. They're unpredictable all the time. So all I can do is wish you luck. Sweet or not, a woman who fights for sport is going to be a handful. No pun intended."

"Yeah, maybe I'm in a weird place right now, and this humidity is messing with my brain," Levi said. "The last thing I should be focused on is a relationship with a woman. I mean, Rhett's got most of my attention, and my team is only winning about fifty percent of their games. Life can change in an instant. I might not even be playing in Minnesota next season."

"This is the first I've heard," Grizz said. "Something going on with your contract?"

"Nothing's going on," Levi said. "That's the problem. They brought me in at base pay, and it goes up by ten percent each year, but other guys are getting bonuses. Like the pitchers and catchers."

Grizz's smile was evident in his voice when he replied. "Well, we're doing all the work. Sorry to break it to you."

"You're lucky you're six states away right now," Levi said. Grizz laughed.

"Tomorrow will be a different story," Levi continued.

"Bring it," Grizz said. "I'll be ready."

"Remember last year's game right after season started?" Levi said. "Minnesota Ice were down by two, and we came back and beat your Pittsburgh butts by three. Thanks to yours truly."

"Remember what I always say," Grizz said. "I never make

the same mistake twice. You should remember that the Pittsburgh Knights made it to the World Series."

"And it was well deserved," Levi said. "You still haven't thanked me for putting the fire under your team's feet."

Grizz laughed. Long and hard.

When Grizz finished, Levi was smiling. "And don't forget the number of players who transferred after. The Knights aren't the same team, and in a few hours, you'll be eating your words."

"Ah." Grizz chuckled. "What's the bet?"

"We win, you wear a dress to the Belltown Parade."

"Deal," Grizz said with a laugh. "And if we win, you send me a picture of your boxer."

CHAPTER 8

"THANKS, MARK," FINLEY said, taking the envelope he was holding out to her. It was her weekly paycheck. She'd already counted up her tips and had given a percentage to the busboy. She'd made a couple of hundred extra dollars covering Jess's shift, plus the seventy-five-dollar tip from Levi Cox had made things add up quickly.

Now all she wanted to do was drop into bed. Levi Cox had his jacket back, and things could return to normal. She glanced at her phone as she headed to the back door. She hadn't replied to Levi's last text because, well, because it made her feel off balance. Besides, she wasn't about to ask him to wait more than an hour in the middle of the night so that he could take her two blocks. He owed her nothing, and she didn't want to owe him anything.

She pushed open the back door of the pub and stepped into the parking lot. Then her breath stalled. Levi's Bronco was parked on the first row, and he was standing near it, his back to her, talking on the phone.

He'd *waited* for her.

Finley's heart thumped.

Should she approach him? Walk past him and hope he didn't see her? No, because then he'd still be waiting for her. And the last thing she wanted him to do was go into the pub and ask about her.

She headed in his direction and walked a little past him, then leaned against the Bronco and folded her arms.

Levi's gaze cut to her. "I've got to go, Grizz."

Laughter came through the phone.

"Shut up," Levi said, then hung up. He put his phone in his pocket and looked over at her. "I didn't see you come out."

His dark-green eyes were unreadable, but one side of his mouth lifted as their gazes connected. And her heart thumped again. Why did he have to be so effortlessly good-looking? It made it hard to focus on much else.

"You didn't have to wait for me," she said.

Levi slipped his hands in his pockets and stepped closer, lowering his voice. "You didn't answer my text, so I didn't have a clear *yes* or *no thanks*."

"No answer usually means *no*," she said. He wasn't wearing his jacket, and she scanned the definition of his arms, his shoulders, although she really shouldn't be checking him out.

"Good to know," Levi said. "But since I'm here, and you're here, can I give you a ride?"

She tilted her head and met those dark-green eyes of his. "I want to know why."

His brows lifted. "Why what?"

"Why you left me a seventy-five-dollar tip," she said, "and why you're out here at one thirty in the morning offering to drive me two blocks. Don't you have anything better to do?"

His mouth twitched. "I don't know, Finley. I'm following instinct, I guess. This is new territory to me."

She held back a smile. It was definitely new territory for

her too. "You mean you don't usually lurk in parking lots in the middle of the night, hoping a waitress will come out and ask for a ride home?"

Levi chuckled. Somehow he'd stepped closer without Finley realizing it.

"This is my first time," he said, scanning her face. "Well, *second* if you count last night."

She looked away then, because she wanted to smile, or maybe swoon, or maybe take his hand and pull him closer. But that would be way too forward.

"If you want a ride," he said in a quiet voice, "I can give you one. Or I could walk you if you're still opposed to getting into my truck. Or you could walk by yourself, but I'd probably follow at a discreet distance, because like I said before, this neighborhood isn't the greatest. Besides, I fly out tomorrow . . . or today, actually . . . so you'll be good and rid of me for a few days."

She met his gaze again. How could he stand there, all hunky and mysterious with those smoldering eyes, and think that she was going to turn him down? "Okay, you can give me a ride, but only because I'm dead on my feet."

Levi smiled, and her stomach fluttered like mad.

He opened the passenger door, and she climbed in. The interior smelled like polished leather, and despite the age of the truck, he'd obviously babied it. She liked the fact that he took care of his things.

When he climbed in the other side, she said, "How did you like your meal?"

"It was perfect," he said, starting the engine. It roared to life, and he backed out of the stall. "Thanks for the recommendation."

"You're so polite."

"Trying to get on your good side, Finley Gray."

The things he said . . . were kind of overwhelming. It was like he spoke his mind, without caring about whether he should be laying it all out.

"Where are you flying to?" she asked. They were already halfway to her place. This drive was going way too fast. Maybe she should have told him to walk her home.

"Pittsburgh," he said. "We're playing the Knights. My old college teammate plays catcher."

"And . . . last night. Was that blond guy a former teammate?"

"Rabbit?" Levi said. He turned the final corner to her apartment building. "Yeah. We were all part of the Six Pack—that's what the media dubbed us. At Belltown University, we won the NCAA championship three years in a row, and six of us were drafted into the Major Leagues the same year. Not everyone had even finished college. But when you get called up, you don't pass that up."

"Did you finish your degree?" Finley asked.

"Yes, ma'am."

"In what?" Nothing in her googling had mentioned what his major had been.

"Uh, I wasn't exactly the academic type, so my degree is in General Studies. Then I went into the accounting tract for the Bachelor's portion. Seems I'm pretty good with money."

Finley smirked. "That's ironic." They'd reached her block, and Levi slowed the Bronco, pulling up to the building.

"I know, I don't make it public knowledge." He shifted the truck into park but didn't shut off the engine. "Are you working tomorrow, or do you get a break?"

"I have tomorrow off," she said. "Best day of the week."

"What are you doing on the Fourth?"

"Monday?" she said. "Working. We can usually see the fireworks from the pub's windows." Was he going to ask her *out*? Would he be back from Pittsburgh already? "What about you?"

"I'll be in Pittsburgh still." He'd put his phone on the console between them. The screen was lighting up with incoming texts, but he ignored them. "We're playing them three nights in a row. I'm assuming the Knights will put on some sort of show after the game."

"Watching fireworks from a baseball field will be better than through a pub window."

"I guess it depends on if we're the winning team or the losing team," he said.

Their gazes connected, and it was surreal to think about, but Finley didn't want this night to end quite yet. "You can come up."

She must have shocked him, because he didn't reply right away.

"I thought you were exhausted."

"I am," she said. Was this a mistake? Too forward? She'd already invited him ... "I'm talking like five minutes tops. This isn't a booty call."

Who knew that Levi Cox could blush. Well, she was now a witness.

"I wouldn't dream of it," he said. "Well, maybe I'd dream of it, but—"

She slugged his arm. "You should stop talking, or I'm going to cancel the invitation."

He shut off the engine and opened his door, and before she could get unbuckled, he was on the other side of the truck, opening her door with a smile.

"You *are* fast, Mr. Florida," she said with a laugh.

Levi held out his hand, and her heart flipped over. She put her hand in his, making it their first contact, and stepped down from the truck.

She wouldn't have minded if he kept holding her hand, but he released it. So she led the way, unable to ignore how the touch of his hand had sent goose bumps racing along her skin. She didn't really know why she'd invited him up to her place. It was in chaos, like usual, but saying goodbye in the truck felt like she was cheating herself out of something. Not that she expected him to kiss her or anything. But she could honestly say that if he did, she wouldn't mind in the least.

She pushed through the front entrance, then walked to the elevators. The glaring fluorescent lights probably drowned out all color in her face, though Levi Cox looked good in any lighting.

"Have you lived here long?" he asked.

"About three years," she said. "I've lived with my dad off and on, but we get along much better living apart."

The elevator dinged open, and she stepped inside, followed by Levi. The small space seemed even smaller with his presence.

"How long have you worked at the pub?"

She shrugged. "Maybe two years now? I've tried those desk jobs, but I can't seem to sit still long enough."

Levi smiled. "Is that why you box?"

The elevator dinged open, and she walked past him without answering. "Here we are." She took out her key and unlocked the door. Then she walked into the apartment and flipped on the lights.

Levi stopped in the doorway.

"You can come in," she said, looking over her shoulder.

"Are you moving or something?" he asked, taking a couple of steps, then shutting the door behind him.

She looked over at the living room and the abundance of furniture. "I'm refinishing some pieces," she said, "then I sell them at the swap meet."

He scanned the furniture. "I don't even have a couch."

She blinked. "What?"

"I don't see the need for one, I guess." He crossed to one of the overstuffed chairs that Finley had recovered in a white-and-blue denim fabric. "You did this yourself?"

"Yeah," she said, coming to stand by him. "It's pretty easy. This chair had a broken leg, so I got my dad to build one for me. He used to manage a furniture shop before he had to retire due to injuring his back. The chair was in good shape despite the broken leg, then I tore off the upholstery and padding and redid everything."

Levi crouched and lifted the chair to inspect the bottom.

"Don't look too closely." She crouched next to him. "That nail is crooked."

"This is cool." He set the chair down and looked over at her. "You're really talented. At a lot of things."

His compliment warmed her through. And she should really put some distance between them because he smelled great, and those dark-green eyes of his were mesmerizing. "Thanks." She straightened. "It's a hobby. YouTube is a great teacher."

He chuckled and walked to the next chair.

It was a strange feeling to watch Levi Cox looking over her upholstery work. Who would have thought a professional baseball player would be so interested in the refurbishing details? He asked more questions, and she answered, trying to keep the conversation casual. Although she wished she'd kept the AC on all day, because her apartment was feeling very hot.

Plus, she probably smelled like the pub. "Do you want a drink?" She moved toward the kitchen. "I've got, um, water or juice or green sludge."

"Green sludge?"

"That's what my dad calls it," she said. "It's a green smoothie."

"Water's fine," he said, his voice closer.

She took out two glasses from the cupboard, glad she'd done the dishes earlier. Opening the freezer door, she took out an ice tray, then cracked it to get the ice loose. She filled both glasses with ice, then added tap water.

"Nothing fancy, but it's cold," she said, turning.

He was standing in the middle of the room, his arms folded, looking at her punching bag that was hanging from the ceiling.

"You really do train here," he said.

"Yep," she said. "Like I said, I'd rather avoid Muscle Mike."

Chapter 9

Levi drank down about half of the ice water. Finley's apartment was warm, and he needed to cool down for other reasons. He was surprised she'd invited him up, and like Grizz had advised him, Levi was determined to take things—whatever those things were—at Finley's pace. Because if it was up to him, he'd probably walk those few steps between them and kiss her.

For now, the ice water would have to suffice.

Her place looked part furniture store, part gym. She was obviously talented, smart, resourceful, and one tough woman, yet her eyes were filled with vulnerability. And Levi was curious as to why. She was a beautiful woman, with plenty of fire, yet she seemed unsure about some things.

He set the glass on the counter and leaned against it. "What's your routine with the bag?"

She had drunk most of her water too, and she set it on the multicolored kitchen table. He wondered if the table was another one of her projects. She moved to the bag and placed a hand on it. "I do five-minute increments. More than twice the length of a round."

"Can you show me?"

She lifted a brow. "You want to try?"

"Sure."

"My gloves might be a little small," she said, looking him up and down. Then she walked to the corner of the room and picked up her gloves from a crate. "These are my newer ones."

She crossed to him, then said, "Hold up your hand."

He sort of liked that she was standing close to him. He lifted his hand, and she slipped on the glove. It was tight. He held up the other hand, and she slipped the other one on.

"Hang on," she said, then went to the crate and pulled out another pair. They looked pretty worn and cracked. Before she pulled them on, she started unbuttoning her shirt. Beneath it, she wore a white tank top.

"Uh, what are you doing?" he asked.

Finley smirked. "I can't get my work shirt ruined." She shrugged out of the shirt, then draped it over a chair.

Levi watched her movements, her easy grace, combined with the strength of her body.

"Keep your eyes on the bag, Mr. Florida," she said with a laugh.

"You're making it hard," he said, not looking away from her.

Her cheeks pinked, but she crossed to the bag and motioned him to join her. "We'll do a warm-up. Go nice and easy."

Levi straightened from the counter. "Okay." He hadn't missed the bruising on her shoulders and arms. "Are you in pain?"

She glanced down at her arms. "Just achy. I'm sort of used to it." Before he could reply, she said, "Wait, I almost forgot. We need music. Helps with the rhythm." She peeled off her gloves, then picked up her phone where she'd left it on the table. She pulled up a playlist, then synched her phone with a speaker on the kitchen counter.

It was some sort of hip-hop, and Levi couldn't have named it, but there was a decent beat.

She moved back to the bag, closer to him. "Pretend like you have an ice pick in your hand, and that you're chipping away at some ice. Not too hard yet."

She demonstrated, and he had to force himself to focus on what her gloves were doing, not the movements of the rest of her body.

Then Finley held the bag. "Okay, you try it while I hold the bag."

Levi slugged it a couple of times, and Finley laughed.

"What's funny?" he asked.

"You have to move your feet, you know, not stand like a statue." She let go of the bag. "Like this."

He watched her hitting and moving, and well, it was better watching her than doing it himself.

"Okay, now your turn." She stopped the bag from moving.

He hit it a few more times, to her approval now. But it was sort of hard to concentrate with her brown eyes on him.

She released the bag and stepped back, then pulled off her gloves.

"You're quitting?" he asked.

"I'm still pretty sore," she said, looking away from him, then picking up her phone and turning down the music.

He took off his gloves and crossed the room and set them in the crate. "So, what got you started boxing?"

She moved around him and walked into the living room. "Because I didn't get in trouble boxing. In soccer, I'd foul and get yellow cards; in basketball more fouls; in softball, one missed catch or bad pitch, and everyone hated you."

He followed her in to the living room and sat on one of the oversized chairs across from the one she picked.

"I also like that boxing is one against one," she said. "Teams have a lot of pressure. If you make a mistake, you let a lot of people down. In boxing, you can only let yourself down."

Levi leaned forward, resting his forearms on his knees. "That makes sense. But fighting isn't for everyone either."

"No." She pulled her legs up onto the chair and tucked them under her. "My dad always told me I had too much energy. It builds and builds, and I have to get rid of it somehow."

Levi quirked a brow. "Maybe you should run marathons."

"Um, no," she said. "So boring."

Levi laughed. "I guess that's a good way to put it. So boxing is . . . an energy release?"

"Among other things." She folded her arms. "Lots of questions, Mr. Florida. What about you? How did you become a baseball star?"

"Energy release?" Levi said.

Finley smirked. "You hold your cards pretty close, Levi Cox."

"I could say the same thing about you."

Her dimples flashed. "*Right* . . . so tell me something about yourself that I can't read on the internet."

"You looked me up?" He felt inordinately pleased at this information.

Her face flushed, and she rose to her feet suddenly. "I had to know whose jacket I ended up with the other night."

He stood as well. "So what did you learn?"

She walked around one of the chairs, trailing her fingers

along the top of the upholstery. "Stuff that doesn't really tell me much about you."

He folded his arms, watching her avoiding his gaze.

She kept walking, kept touching the furniture. Then she turned. She eyed him for a moment.

He moved around the couch that separated them. She didn't move away as he approached. When he stopped in front of her, she looked up at him. "What do you want to know?" he asked.

Her brown eyes were warm and curious, and he liked that she wasn't on the other side of the room. That she was close enough that he could easily lean down and kiss her.

"Stuff that you like, maybe?" she said.

Levi scanned her face, her eyes, her nose, her lips. "I like your dimples."

Her lips parted as if she were about to protest, then she slugged him.

He laughed and rubbed his arm.

"Something about *you*," she said, resting her hands on her hips. "Something I can't find on Google."

"Like what?"

"Um, what's your favorite color?"

He raised his brows.

"I'm serious."

He gazed at her for a second before saying, "Gray."

"No one's favorite color is gray." Then her cheeks pinked. "Oh."

Finley tried to slug his arm again, but he caught her hand. "You've got to stop doing that," he said.

She tugged against his hold, but he held fast.

"Why?" Her voice was breathless.

"Because it's making me think you like me." He stepped closer, and she stopped trying to pull her hand away. "You know, like you can't stop yourself from touching me," he continued. "So you slug me, hoping that I'll take you in my arms. And maybe kiss you."

"Is *that* what it means?" She took a small step back, but she was smiling.

"You tell me."

She bit her lip, and he wanted to throw Grizz's advice out the window. Instead, Levi rested his free hand on her hip. Her brows lifted, but she didn't move.

"Maybe I do like you, maybe I don't," she said. "It's hard to tell when you don't give me a lot of space."

He smiled, then he released her hand and put his other hand on her other hip. They weren't touching any other place, except for his hands on her hips.

She tilted her head, her brown eyes warm. "Are you going to kiss me, Levi Cox?"

"Do you want me to?"

Her gaze moved to his mouth, and his pulse went into overdrive.

When she placed her hands on his shoulders, he hoped that meant her answer was *yes*. But he couldn't be positive with a woman like Finley Gray.

He leaned down and kissed her cheek, right on her dimple. She didn't move away, so he lingered. Her breathing was fast, matching his own.

"What are you doing, Mr. Florida?" she whispered.

"Kissing your cheek," he whispered back.

"I think you're doing more than that."

He smiled, but he didn't pull away. "You're very observant."

"I'm also kind of sweaty." Her fingers brushed against his neck. "And I smell like a pub."

"I don't mind sweat," he whispered. "Or the pub." He felt

her smile. So he pressed his mouth against the edge of her lips. He was getting closer. "I smell raspberries."

She lifted a hand and touched her hair. "The scent of my shampoo survived."

He kissed the other side of her mouth. "Do you want me to stop?"

She exhaled. "No."

He slid his hands around her waist and drew her close, their bodies finally touching. He'd been right. She was plenty soft. Her hands moved behind his neck and into his hair, and it was all the invitation he needed. Levi pressed his mouth against hers.

Her lips parted beneath his, and she welcomed his kiss, matching her own desire with his. Encouraged, he pulled her closer, kissing her harder, tasting more of her. She gripped the fabric of his T-shirt and kissed him back.

Levi ran his hands up her back as he kissed her. He trailed his fingers over the bare skin of her shoulders, then along her neck. She shivered against him, and everything inside of him buzzed. His heart was racing like mad, and his thoughts were spinning in all kinds of crazy directions. He wanted more. He cradled her face and angled his mouth to deepen his kiss.

Finley seemed to melt against him. Her hands skimmed over his shoulders, then down his biceps. He was pretty sure he had goose bumps, mixed with fire in his veins. Her touch was making him ignite. Was that possible?

Levi knew he had to slow things down, cool things off. He moved his hands behind her neck and slowed the kissing. Her arms went around his waist, anchoring them together. Levi kissed the edge of her mouth, then her jaw, then lower, down her neck, where her pulse was throbbing.

"Finley," he whispered against her skin. "I think my five minutes are up."

"Definitely up," she whispered.

"So . . ." he began. "I'll be back in town Thursday to play the Iowa Devils. Do you want to come to my game?"

She drew away slightly and met his gaze with a half smile.

It only made him want to kiss her again.

"You want me to be a fan girl?"

He chuckled. "I want to see you again. Come to my game, and then we'll go do something after."

Her brows raised. "Are you going to try to kiss me again?"

"I am." He pressed his lips on her cheek, then murmured, "Are you working that night?"

"Yes, but I can try to switch my shift for earlier in the day."

"Then do it." He kissed the edge of her jaw.

She ran her hands up his sides, then released him and stepped away. "Maybe. I'll let you know."

He grasped her hand and linked their fingers.

"Goodbye, Levi," she said, arching a brow.

"Okay, I'm leaving." He slid his hand from hers, and he turned toward the door. He opened it and went out, then shut it without looking back. Because it would only make it harder to leave.

CHAPTER 10

"WHAT'S WITH ALL the questions about baseball?" Finley's dad asked over the phone.

"I'm curious, that's all," she said into her headphones as she ran on her treadmill. "The game's on right now."

"The game?"

"You know, the Minnesota Ice," she said. "They're playing the Pittsburgh Knights."

"I know who they're playing, but I'm surprised *you* do."

Finley shrugged even though her dad couldn't see her. It was Wednesday night, and Levi had been texting her several times a day over the past few days. Most of the texts had been short, flirtatious. Apparently he hadn't forgotten their kiss in her apartment either. Finley turned the fan on her treadmill up a notch. Thinking of how Levi Cox had kissed her made her overheat.

"Fin?" her dad prompted. "Are you okay?"

She knew that voice—his *concerned parent* voice—and she didn't want the twenty questions that would only annoy her. So maybe she should tell him the truth. "I'm fine, Dad," she said. "Here's the thing. I need to tell you something, but I don't want you blowing it out of proportion."

"When have I ever done such a thing?" he asked.

Finley laughed. "You're kidding, right? Remember prom my junior year? You borrowed army fatigues from your friend. You answered the door wearing them and holding a water pistol. I almost got left at the doorstep."

Her dad chuckled. No remorse there. "I didn't want Robby to think he could take advantage of my little girl."

"Oh, he got the message," Finley said. She could look back now and laugh, but at the time she'd been mortified. "He never asked me out again. And come to think of it, I didn't date the rest of my junior year."

"None of those guys were good enough for you anyway, honey," her dad said. Good ole, trusty Dad.

"Here's the thing, Dad," she said. "I'm going out with Levi Cox tomorrow night."

Her dad didn't say anything for a moment.

"You know, the baseball player—"

"I know who he is," her dad snapped. "Professional athletes are all the same, I tell you. They use women and—"

"Dad," Finley cut in. "Not all pro athletes are the same."

"How do you know Cox?" her dad shot out.

"Um, he was in the pub last week with some other players, and—"

"He picked you up? At a *bar*?"

"I was working, at the pub where I'm *employed*, Dad."

"I don't like it," her dad said. "Hang on, I'm texting Brad. I want to see if Levi Cox has a record."

Finley's heart sank. Not only because it might be true that Levi had a record, but that her dad's best friend, Brad Hampton, was a cop. And Hampton would be only too happy to give more details on the public records to her dad.

"Dad," Finley said. "I'm not seventeen anymore."

"I don't care how old you are," he said. "You're still my daughter. Brad just texted back. He's looking up Cox."

Finley bit back a groan and paced the floor, her body not cooling off one bit because of the conversation with her dad. Of course she wanted to know if Levi had a record, but it felt cheap and underhanded to find out this way. It was something she should be able to ask him about. Right? She walked into the kitchen and downed a glass of water.

"Oh boy," her dad said. "There's a bunch of stuff here."

Finley dropped onto a kitchen chair. She rested her head on her hand. "What is it?"

"Plenty of juvie incidents," he said. "Those records are sealed, but you can still see that there were things going on. And a few years ago, an altercation with another man. Only two years ago, Cox was in another altercation and charged with disorderly conduct and obstruction of justice. That's a felony."

Finley exhaled. She had to think straight. "What does it say?"

"Well, I don't have the police report, just the list of charges that were filed."

She rubbed her forehead. "I seriously doubt that if Levi Cox were found guilty of a felony, he'd still have his baseball contract."

"You'd be surprised," her dad said. "Those professional athletes get away with a ton. Unless they're charged with murder, they get fined. Domestic abuse, theft, DUIs, all get swept under the rug."

Finley stood from the table and paced the kitchen. "Obstruction of justice is a far cry from that other stuff. You know how cops are."

Her dad wouldn't budge an inch. "Fin, be smart."

She exhaled. "I'll talk to him. Find out what happened."

"Before you go out with him," her dad said. "Promise?"

"Promise." When she hung up with her dad, the butterflies that had been spinning inside her since Levi had kissed her had turned into lead.

The sound of the baseball game on the TV in the living room cut into her thoughts. She walked into the living room and stood a few feet in front of the TV. The Knights were in the field, and the Minnesota Ice were up to bat. One out. No one on base. She'd watched all of Levi's games since Sunday night, pulling them up online after she got off work at the pub. Today she'd worked the early shift, so she was watching this one live.

She knew the batting rotation well enough to know Levi should be up in two more. The current player hit a two-base run. Then the next player struck out.

One out. One man on second. Levi approached the home plate.

Finley was familiar with his routine by now too; it was always the same. He'd tap his helmet, then rotate his shoulders, followed by swinging the bat into a wide arc, which ended as he positioned the bat almost behind his head.

Strike.

It was a sloppy swing; even Finley could see that.

She took a step closer to the TV. Levi seemed agitated about something. He went through his batting routine twice before stepping up to the plate again. The announcer mentioned something about words said between Levi and the Knights pitcher, Young. But the announcer didn't seem to have any real information, only speculation.

The Knights pitcher threw a wild ball, and it almost hit Levi. He jumped back and took a couple of steps forward, as if he was going to rush the pitcher's mound.

The catcher, who Finley knew was his college teammate

Grizz, stood and pushed up his catcher's mask. Grizz's bearded face showed he wasn't happy about Levi's actions.

Levi turned on Grizz, and the ump stepped between them. Words had been said, at the very least.

Finley realized she was clenching her teeth as she watched. "Just play the game, Levi," she said to the TV. Sunday and Tuesday's games hadn't been this heated. And with her dad's words ringing in her head about Levi's record, Finley was keyed up too.

She held her breath as the next pitch was thrown.

Levi swung hard and connected with the ball. It sailed above the shortstop's head and landed between right field and centerfield. The centerfielder reached the ball first, grabbed it, and chucked it to second. The runner on second returned to his base. Meanwhile, Levi sprinted, making it to first easily.

The next batter swaggered up to the plate. Kaelin, or Number Nine as he was called, had already hit a home run in the second inning, and the announcer was making predictions on a repeat performance. But the pitcher seemed determined to walk Kaelin.

Ball one.

Ball two.

Ball three.

The runner on second led off and sprinted to third. Grizz threw a straight line to third, and the runner was tagged out. Levi had run to second without any interference.

Two outs.

Kaelin scuffed his cleats next to the home plate, then went into his stance. The next pitch was high, but Kaelin swung.

Strike one.

As Grizz threw the ball back to Young, Levi took off,

sprinting for third. The pitcher caught the ball, then threw to third. A split second too late. Levi was safe.

Finley squeezed her hands together. "Get home, Levi," she whispered. "Shake off whatever's going on."

Another pitch. Kaelin swung low.

Strike two.

"Full count!" the ump called.

Grizz threw the ball back, and the pitcher fumbled the catch. Levi had already led off third base, and now he ran toward home.

The play seemed to slow down as the pitcher recovered the ball and rotated to throw to Grizz. But instead of throwing to the catcher, Young threw the ball at Levi's thigh. The ball struck its mark. Levi went down in a dive, but he managed to stretch out and touch home plate with his hand before rolling over and grabbing his leg.

Finley gasped and covered her mouth.

But Levi didn't stay down for long. In seconds, he was on his feet, running straight toward the pitcher. Then it seemed as if the entire field had erupted as the dugouts emptied of baseball players. The Ice and the Knights all ran toward each other.

"And the benches have cleared!" the announcer said. "Cox is going after Young!"

Some players were swinging punches, and others were trying to pull apart players.

Finley stared at the brawl. Of course she knew there were baseball brawls that happened. It was all part of the game, when a player was hit by a pitcher, or . . .

Two Minnesota Ice players propelled Levi off the field, and the other skirmishes were broken up. Within minutes, the field had cleared, and order seemed to be restored, but there was a higher tension to the game. The announcer kept talking about Levi Cox and how there had been words between the Knights pitcher and Levi at some previous point.

A new pitcher was brought in to pitch out the rest of the inning.

Finley sank onto a half-finished chair. The brawl didn't bother her. And Levi's part didn't bother her on the basic level. But her dad's voice was still in her mind.

Sure enough, her phone rang.

"Hi, Dad," she said.

"Are you still watching?"

"Yes."

"You'd better speak to him before you see him again," he said. "*If* you do see him again. The guy's a hothead. I called Randall. He's been following the Ice for years, knows everything about every player."

Finley closed her eyes as she listened to her dad talk about what his friend Randall had said about Levi Cox. Some of it she knew from the internet. Some of it was new. Like how his mom was in jail and how his brother was only his half-brother. "He's got bad blood, Fin."

"I don't believe in bad blood," Finley said, although she didn't sound convincing to herself, let alone to her dad. "He was in foster care, like a lot of kids in this country. He's beaten the odds. Yeah, maybe he started a brawl, but the pitcher deliberately targeted him. Besides, I'll bet I can pull up dozens of YouTube videos right now on baseball brawls. And I can guarantee that Levi Cox didn't start all of them."

Her dad went silent for a moment. "Call me after you talk to him."

She puffed out a breath. "I will." She hung up and turned off her phone. If her dad called back, she didn't want to deal with any more ranting. She watched the rest of the game.

Things seemed to have settled down, probably helped by the fact that the Minnesota Ice won.

Finley spent the next hour doing increments of boxing in her kitchen. She decided that if Levi texted her after the game, she'd call him. But she hated to confront him about his record after such a tense game. Maybe to him it wasn't a big deal.

By the time Finley had worn herself out, there was no text from Levi. Not that she could expect anything from him, but he'd texted her soon after his games on other nights. She scrolled through their texting strand. After reading it, she made a decision. She'd be honest and blunt and let him take it from there.

Congrats on the win, Mr. Florida. Hope you're okay after that brawl. She took a deep breath and continued typing. *So I mentioned to my dad that we were going out tomorrow night, and he sent me stuff about your past. If you can call me when you have a chance, that would be great.*

Finley reread the text, then hit SEND. She waited for a couple of minutes; not that she expected her phone to ring, but maybe he'd text back that he'd call her soon?

Thirty minutes later, he still hadn't replied. Finley got in the shower, then made a protein shake. Still nothing from Levi. She wasn't sure if they were flying back tonight or in the morning. Maybe he was on a plane? Maybe his phone was off? Maybe she was reading too much into his intentions about her, and she'd stepped into his personal space.

She must have fallen asleep on one of her couches with her cell phone because she woke to it ringing. The screen was lit up with Levi's name, and it took Finley a second to realize it was two in the morning.

"Hello?" she answered, her voice raspy.

"Are you home?" Levi asked.

"Um..." She sat up. "Yeah, of course."

"Okay, I'm coming up." The phone went dead.

Finley stared at the screen. Before she could comprehend that Levi was here, at her apartment, at two in the morning, a knock sounded at the door.

Chapter 11

Levi's decision-making had been a bit rash the past few days, and that was only confirmed when Finley answered the door. She'd obviously been asleep when he'd called. She was wearing a tank top and some sort of pajama shorts. She wore no makeup, which made her look younger and more vulnerable, and her hair was a tumble of black over her shoulders.

But seeing her again after four days also confirmed his growing interest in her, not to mention the strength of his attraction. Her minimal clothing wasn't helping in that department.

"Sorry to wake you," he said.

She blinked as if she was still trying to wake up. "Are you okay? That looks painful." She stepped closer and touched his cheek, right below the bruising that had started to form around his eye.

The Knights pitcher had thrown him a good one, but Levi had returned the favor. It had been a frustrating game all the way around. Levi and Grizz had ended the night on good terms, but their argument after the game hadn't been pleasant. Then Levi had joined his team in the locker room, where they were rushing to shower, pack up, and get on the plane.

When he'd seen Finley's text, Levi knew exactly what was going on. And it wasn't something to be discussed over the phone. He'd dated a woman for about four months at Belltown, then he had told her about his past, his criminal convictions, his juvie record. Their relationship had ended that same night. Since then, he'd never shared his past with anyone he'd dated, telling himself that if things got serious, then he would. Things had never gotten serious.

Yet, before much could really get started with Finley, she was already asking. Courtesy of her dad, and likely the internet, which painted a one-sided picture.

Finley had obviously showered before falling asleep, because her raspberry scent washed over Levi. And her touching his face was making his heart race and his thoughts jumble.

"I'm okay," he said, grasping her wrist and moving her hand away. "I came to talk to you in person . . . about my past."

Her eyes were clearer now, more awake, and she nodded. "Come in. I've got my own stash of tea bags now."

"Finley, you don't have to. Really."

But she grabbed his hand and led him into the kitchen.

"Sit." She pointed at a chair.

Next thing he knew, she was moving about the kitchen, steeping a tea bag, then bringing it to him.

"Tilt your head back," she said. "And close your eyes."

Even with his eyes closed, he was aware of her every movement, her every touch as she positioned the tea bag below his eye, then laid a warm cloth on top of it. What he wanted to do was pull her onto his lap and bury his face in her neck. Breathe her in. Feel her arms about him. But he didn't know if she'd want to see him anymore after he divulged his past. And he didn't want to take advantage of her.

So he waited. After a few minutes, he removed the cloth and tea bag. "Thank you," he said.

Finley was sitting across the table from him. "Do you want something to drink? Are you hungry?"

"I'm good," he said. "I got your text, and I didn't want to explain over the phone." He shifted in his chair. "Can we sit on one of the softer chairs in the living room so I can stretch out my leg?"

"Oh, that's right," she said. "You got nailed in the thigh. Can you walk okay?"

He held back a smile, wishing his heart felt lighter. "I can walk fine. Just sore."

"Do you want a tea bag on your leg?"

"Um, no." He definitely couldn't handle the event of her touching his thigh.

Finley rose from the chair and moved into the living room, turning on a lamp as she went. She sat in one of the overstuffed chairs, and he took one of the couches.

"I'm sorry that I stressed you out," Finley said. "I told my dad . . . maybe that was a mistake, but he went off on a major tangent."

"I get it," he said. "And don't apologize. I'm not trying to hide anything. That stuff isn't really a first-date conversation."

Finley nodded and absently started to braid her hair. "Yeah, true."

"And I didn't realize how late it was." He scanned the room. She'd added another piece of furniture since he was last here. "You know I was a foster kid growing up?"

"Yeah, you and your brother."

"Rhett is my half-brother," he said. "We have different dads, the same mom. When Rhett was about two, and I was about seven, my mom was put in jail for dealing drugs. She was part of a pretty major drug and prostitution ring."

He didn't want to feel Finley's pity, but he felt it anyway. "I'm sorry, Levi."

He shrugged. It was a long time ago. Water under the bridge, and all the clichés. "I barely remember her. My brother and I were kept together for a couple of years, but then we started getting split up. I went a little crazy when that happened. Ran away multiple times, trying to find him. Finally the state put us back together contingent on my behavior."

Finley was staring at him, and he could only guess what was going through her mind.

"Bottom line, my brother and I are opposites," Levi continued, dumping it all out at once. "Rhett's brainy, an introvert too, stayed in the awkward stage well past middle school, and well, he got bullied. So I was his protector. Got into lots of fights. Not only in school, but in whatever foster home we were in. Mostly with the siblings of the families. Once with a foster dad. Got sent to juvie for that."

"For standing up for your brother?" she asked, her tone incredulous.

"For doing it the wrong way," Levi said. "I used my fists instead of my words." He adjusted his leg so that it wasn't throbbing quite so much. He tried to hide his wince but failed.

Finley stood and moved to the couch. "Here, put your leg on my lap." She sat at the other end and propped up his foot across her lap.

When the pinch of pain from the movement subsided, he said, "As a kid, I guess I could sort of justify things—troubled foster kid, you know. But as an adult I have no excuses, unless you count a temper."

Finley didn't say anything, didn't look at him.

"A couple of years ago, I got arrested at a pub downtown. Not far from yours," he said. "I was there with some teammates, and I didn't like how they were talking to one of the waitresses. We got into an argument, and I was shoved first. I hit back. But I wouldn't tell the police officer who instigated the fight. So I was charged with obstruction of justice."

Finley moved her gaze to meet his. "What about your teammate?"

"Everyone was cited," Levi said. "The first guy doesn't even play baseball anymore. I haven't gone to a pub or a bar in that area since. Until last week, when I went with Rabbit and his teammates."

Finley set her hand on his ankle, and the warmth of her fingers was like a balm. "What about the brawl? Does that happen often?"

"More than I'd like," he said. "I can't stand pitchers who are crooked. Too many great players have been injured or worse."

Her hand moved a couple of inches. "My dad wants me to call him after I talk to you. He has a friend who is a huge fan of the Minnesota Ice, who filled in my dad on a bunch of stuff. He also has a friend who's a cop."

Levi nodded. "No problem. I can talk to your dad too, if you want."

"Really?"

"Really," he said. "Give him my number, or better yet, bring him to the game."

Finley exhaled. "I don't know if that's such a good idea."

"The game, or bringing your dad?"

She didn't say anything.

Levi moved his leg off her lap, and despite the pain, he put both feet on the ground. "The tickets will be there. I'd love you to come. Bring your dad if you want. It's your decision, Finley."

She wasn't looking at him, but she nodded.

Levi pushed up from the couch and stood. His heart was

literally hurting, and he didn't think he could deal with any more time in Finley's presence knowing that he'd let her down. "I'm really sorry you had to find out about me the hard way. And I'm sorry I woke you up. Maybe the Knights pitcher hit me harder than I thought."

He moved to the door and opened it. Putting distance between himself and Finley was the best idea right now, because he was weak. Weak enough to beg her to not hold his record against him, to promise that he was a better man than a list of charges. But if he had to convince her, then that was broken. She'd have to decide herself. Both of them knew that a position on a professional sports team and a large paycheck didn't make up for the more serious things in life.

Levi shut the door behind him quietly. He figured if he were to bet whether she'd be at the game, he'd lose badly. When a girl's father was involved, it took things to the next level on hyper speed. And that's what had just happened with Finley.

He walked down the stairs, then pushed through the exit door, leaving the apartment building. He climbed into the Bronco, which he'd parked at the curb. A good night's sleep was what he needed. Get through Thursday night's game, and then the following day, he'd be in Belltown for the parade. He'd get his head screwed on straight with the Six Pack. And seeing Rhett would be good too—Levi could determine for himself whether his brother was really doing okay.

He didn't want to think too deeply about Finley, because if he let his mind dwell on her, he wouldn't be able to stop the regrets. A lifetime of regrets. And none of it he could change.

Fourteen hours later, he was on the field, warming up with his team. His leg was still sore, but he wouldn't let that be an issue in the game. He'd received dozens of texts from the Six Pack, checking in on him, first with concern. Then, as always, the concern changed to razzing and everyone making predictions on their various games tonight. Grizz had a bye for two days, but all the others were playing.

Levi tossed the ball to other infielders, every so often checking the seats that were for Finley and her dad. The stadium had started to fill, but the seats remained empty. Levi tried to shake the worry from his thoughts, but it was like a dead weight in his mind. He knew that if she didn't come tonight, he'd probably never see her again.

It wasn't like he could show up at the pub or knock on her apartment door. He'd told her everything. Now she was the one with the decision to make. If he were a father . . . he didn't know how he'd react to his daughter dating a Levi Cox.

He blew out a breath as the coaches called the players to the dugout for a final word before they retook the field and the game began. The Iowa Devils were picked to win, but Levi had watched game film on them earlier that day. He'd found a few loopholes that he planned to take advantage of.

And . . . there it was. The pitcher he hoped he didn't have to hit against—Ramie. The guy was up to bat first.

Levi glanced again at the two empty seats, then dragged his gaze away to focus on the batter. Ramie arched his back when he stepped up to the home plate—ridiculous. Then he spit in the dirt right next to the catcher. Levi rested his hands on his knees, watching every movement from Ramie.

"Come on, Scrubs," Levi hollered at the Minnesota Ice pitcher. "Strike out The Ram."

Scrubs had been having a good month, and Levi needed it to continue. Whether Finley showed up at the game or not, Levi didn't want to lose to the bottom-feeder Devils.

Strike.

"Way to go, Scrubs," Levi called out. "Throw 'im another one!"

The Ram looked over at Levi.

"You listening to *me*?" Levi mocked. "Keep your eye on the ball, boy."

The Ram narrowed his eyes, then went through his prissy routine.

Strike two!

"Yeah!" Levi shouted. "Nice job, pitch!"

Scrubs tipped his hat at Levi.

"What are you waiting for, Ram?" Levi called. "Game's already started."

The Ram swung at the next pitch. It was a hardline drive right about four feet above Levi's head. He took two steps back, then jumped. The ball smacked into his mitt with a solid thud.

"Out!" the ump yelled.

"Bring it, Scrubs!" Levi called. So far, so good. Then he glanced toward the two seats again, and this time he paused. Two teenagers sat in the seats. Either Finley had given the tickets away, or someone had moved into them, thinking they were empty.

Disappointment settled deep into Levi's gut. He snapped his gaze back to the field as Scrubs threw a low pitch.

Ball one.

Chapter 12

THE BOTTOM OF the fifth inning, and Levi was up to bat. Finley might not have gone to the game, but she couldn't stop herself from watching it. Levi had already scored in two previous innings, but so had the Devils. Current score: Minnesota Ice 7, Devils 8. It was a high scoring game, and both the energy and tension were at a max.

A new pitcher was on the mound—Ramie, or The Ram, as the announcers referred to him. Finley could see that Levi was agitated, and she pretended it had nothing to do with her or their conversation in the middle of the night.

After talking to her dad this morning, she'd decided to take his advice. Let some time pass. A few days, a week or two, then see how she still felt. At least her dad had been sensitive to *her* feelings and hadn't been too overbearing in demanding that she ditch Levi. Although it wasn't too hard to read between the lines where her dad was concerned. The tone of his voice said everything his words didn't.

Strike.

"Dang it, Levi," Finley muttered. "Get a piece of that thing." Her heart rate rose a couple of notches. Happened every time he stepped up to the home plate.

"There's no love lost between Levi and Ramie," the announcer said. "Last year, Ramie hit Scrubs on his helmet, knocking him out. Levi Cox went after Ramie, starting a brawl."

Another brawl with a pitcher?

She bit her lip as Ramie pitched and Levi swung.

"Strike two!" the ump called.

"Come on," Finley said. "*Hit the ball.*"

Ramie went into his pitcher's windup and threw.

Levi swung again, and this time, it was a short grounder. Stopping between the home plate and the pitcher's mound. Levi took off, and the crowd yelled as he raced against time.

"Go!" Finley yelled at the TV.

As if Levi had heard her, he crossed first base a half second before the ball.

"Cox on base," the announcer said. "Now let's see what Makin can do. He's struggled in this game, but the Minnesota Ice currently have the momentum."

The camera focused on the next batter.

Ramie threw a low pitch, and the catcher fumbled the ball before getting hold of it. Suddenly the camera panned to second base.

"Cox is going for it!" the announcer yelled. "Look at that dive, folks. And . . . *he's safe.* That right there is how he got the nickname Steal."

Finley's heart had leapt into her throat, and she watched as Levi picked himself off the ground and brushed dirt from his jersey. The front of his entire uniform was covered in dirt, and Finley couldn't help but think of his bruised face and thigh from yesterday's game. Yet he'd ignored all that and made the play.

The camera returned to the batter, although the

announcer was still sharing accolades about Levi Cox's base stealing.

He deserved those accolades. He'd made an incredible play, a result of hard work and sheer determination. Finley had been a witness to his ball playing for several games now. Levi hadn't asked to be born to a druggie mom. He hadn't asked to be abandoned by his dad. Levi hadn't chosen to live in foster care until he was the legal age of eighteen. Despite his mistakes, his heart had been in the right place all along. Focused on his brother and focused on using baseball to make something of himself.

Finley picked up her cell phone and called her dad. "I'm going to the game. Meet me there if you want. I'd love to introduce you to Levi."

Her father didn't say anything for a moment.

Finley waited. He was stubborn, but she was more stubborn.

"I'll pick you up on the way," he finally said.

Finley blinked against the burning in her eyes. "Thanks, Dad."

Thirty minutes later, Finley led the way to their seats at the baseball stadium. Two teenaged boys were sitting there, but her dad made quick work of shooing them out.

Finley sat down as the top of the seventh inning started. Levi was tossing the ball to the infielders. When he next caught it, he threw it to the pitcher.

"That's Bryce Trout pitching," her dad said. "He's the big closer. They call him Big T."

Finley nodded, listening to her dad but more focused on Levi. They were sitting only a few rows up from the field, and she knew Levi would be able to see her if he looked in their direction. What would he think of her showing up so late?

"I watched Big T pitch a no-hitter game a couple of years ago," her dad added.

The first batter on the Devils walked up to the home plate. Finley's dad leaned forward, focusing on the play.

Finley watched Levi. His clothing was stained with dirt, and she could see the bruising around his eye at this distance. He said something to the pitcher, but she couldn't hear it.

Big T threw the ball, fast and smooth over home plate.

"Strike one!" the ump called.

The home crowd cheered, and the energy of the game buzzed about Finley.

Her dad was talking about the pitcher and his career, but Finley was watching Levi again. He spoke to the shortstop, who nodded, then Levi yelled something to the pitcher.

Big T went into his windup and threw another fastball.

"Strike two!"

Finley clapped and cheered along with the rest of the crowd.

Big T nodded at the catcher, then threw again. But the ball was high.

"Ball one!"

The crowd groaned, and some guys a few rows above them started heckling the pitcher.

Finley turned to stare them down, and her dad put a hand on her arm. "It's just baseball, honey. Ignore them."

She exhaled and turned back around as Big T's pitch crossed the plate.

"Strike three!" the ump called.

"Yes!" her dad said. "Big T's still got it!"

The batter stalked back to the Devil's dugout. Another batter strode toward the plate, and Finley looked over at Levi again. He smacked his mitt against his knee and rotated his neck.

Then his gaze cut to where she was sitting.

Finley inhaled as their eyes met. She was close enough to make no mistake that he'd seen her. Levi looked at her dad, then back to her.

Should she wave? Smile?

The pitcher went into the windup, and Levi's attention was diverted. But Finley could swear she'd seen his expression relax a bit. Or maybe she'd imagined it.

"Ball one," the umpire called.

"Come on, Big T, find the sweet spot!" Levi called to the pitcher.

Finley had watched Levi yell things to the pitcher, but for some reason, she could hear him now. Maybe her ears had zoned in on his voice or something.

Levi glanced up at her again, and this time he winked.

Heat rushed through her at that simple acknowledgment. There was no denying it now. Levi knew she was here, and he seemed pleased. She bit the inside of her lip to stop herself from grinning like a fool.

The Minnesota Ice held the Devils' scoring off, and in the next inning, Scrubs got a home run, tying the game. Levi hit a two-base run, then stole the rest of the bases and scored. Finley wasn't surprised, and she jumped to her feet with the rest of the crowd as he ran across home plate.

His teammates erupted from the dugout to congratulate him for scoring the point that finally put them ahead of the Devils. Levi was swallowed up in the mass of players, and she didn't see him again until he came out onto the field at the bottom of the eighth.

No one scored again, and the Minnesota Ice won the game by one run. Finley stood and cheered with her dad and the crowd. She watched as the team came out of the dugout, and people were let onto the field to get balls and shirts signed.

Levi was among the players giving autographs. She wondered if spectators had to have some sort of pass.

"Come on, Dad," Finley said. "Come and meet Levi."

"Are you sure?" her dad asked.

It might sound like a simple question, but Finley knew he was asking much, much more.

"I'm sure," she said.

So they waded through the crowd, moving in the opposite direction until they got to the security gate.

"Hi," Finley said to the security officer. "Do you need some sort of special pass to meet a player?"

"You do," the security guy said, eyeing her and her dad.

"Levi Cox gave us these tickets," her dad said, holding out the tickets they'd gotten at will call.

"I don't think that's what he meant," Finley told her dad.

"Hang on, Jack," someone said. "They're with me."

Finley looked over and saw Levi walking toward them. Her knees went all wobbly, and she found herself grinning like a fool after all. Up close, she could see that Levi wore his uniform very well, and despite the perspiration and dirt, she'd never found him more attractive than at this moment. The bruising about his eye had faded. And the scruff along his chin and jaw only made him look sexier.

The security guard waved them through, and Levi held out his hand to her dad.

As the two men shook hands, Finley said, "Levi, this is my dad, Charlie Gray."

"Nice to meet you, Mr. Gray," Levi said.

"Charlie's fine," her dad said.

That alone gave Finley hope. Her dad wouldn't have said that if he didn't think Levi Cox was worth something.

"Hope the seats were good?" Levi asked, his dark-green gaze moving to Finley.

She saw the questions in his eyes, and the hope, and it only made a small fire ignite in her belly.

"They were amazing," Finley said. "Thank you."

"Sorry we were a bit late," her dad said, surprising Finley. "Traffic."

Levi smiled, and Finley knew he wasn't fooled.

"No worries," Levi said. "The end is always the best anyway."

Her dad chuckled, and Finley wanted to hug him. Or hug both men. After Levi showered, of course; but in truth, she didn't mind the sweat.

"That's quite a shiner," her dad said to Levi. "That from Young?"

"Yeah, he got me good," Levi said. His gaze was on her again, and Finley sort of wished she could talk to him privately.

"Some of the guys are going over to the Blue Crow pub," Levi said, looking over at her father. "Do you want to join us?"

Her dad's eyes about bugged out. "Me too?"

"Of course," Levi said in an easy tone, clapping his hand on her dad's shoulder. "I'm sure they'd love to hear your take on the game."

Finley was pretty sure she fell in love with Levi right on the spot.

Her dad chuckled. "I couldn't add much, not like my friend Randall could. But we'd love to come."

Finley almost kissed her dad.

"Great," Levi said. "Give us about thirty minutes. You'll thank us for showering later. We've got a section reserved under my name at the Blue Crow."

Which meant that Levi had set this up in advance of knowing whether she was coming.

Finley slipped her hands in her shorts pockets so that she

wouldn't spontaneously throw her arms around Levi's neck. Yes, her dad was pleased, but she didn't want to shock him, or Levi, with PDA.

"Sounds great," her dad said.

"Okay then, see you soon," Levi said.

His gaze was on her once again, and she could only nod, because her mind was a little fuzzy. Levi Cox had invited her and her dad to dinner with his teammates. Things had just moved up on the legit relationship scale.

Her dad said goodbye and maybe something else. As Finley watched Levi rejoin the crowd of hopefuls, her dad speculated about the other players who might show up at the pub. As for Finley, she didn't care who else came. Levi would be there, and that's all that mattered.

She and her dad walked to his car through the dispersing crowd. On the drive over to the pub, her dad said, "He seems like a decent guy."

Finley nodded. This was all so surreal. She'd almost not even come to the game. And now here her dad was, excited to spend more time with him, and Finley was about to hang out with Levi's teammates.

"I mean, he did have a rough upbringing," he said. "Other kids get into trouble with privileged lives. Levi Cox had to dig things out of the dirt."

The admiration was evident in her dad's tone, and for that Finley was grateful. "I agree, Dad," she said. "Thanks for giving him a chance." She leaned over and kissed her dad's cheek as he parked behind the pub.

Her dad smiled, his face a bit flushed.

"Should we wait for them to arrive in the parking lot, or go inside?" Finley asked.

"Let's wait here," her dad said.

About twenty minutes later, Levi's Bronco pulled in, followed by a black Suburban.

"Look at that, there they are," her dad said.

Sure enough, several Ice players climbed out of a black Suburban. Levi and the pitcher, Bryce Trout, exited the Bronco.

Levi was wearing a plain white T-shirt and faded jeans. He looked fresh from the shower, and the faded bruise on his face only made him look like somebody's hero. She should probably get out of the car now, or she'd continue to melt against the car seat as she stared at Levi.

Finley opened her door and climbed out. Ready or not, it was time.

CHAPTER 13

LEVI INTRODUCED FINLEY and her dad to Big T, Scrubs, Number Nine, and the others as they walked to the pub entrance. There were eight in all, and good thing the pub had reserved tables, because the place was packed. Not Levi's ideal situation, but Charlie Gray had seemed pleased enough with the invite.

Besides, Levi had been hoping that Finley would bring her dad. Levi was relieved she'd finally showed up at the game, and bringing her dad seemed to be a very good sign. Levi glanced over at Charlie as he talked to Big T. Charlie's hair was mostly black, peppered with some white, and he was a heavy-set man, but not in a sloppy way. He looked like a former football player, and his broad shoulders still had plenty of presence.

Charlie's eyes were also brown, but a lighter brown than Finley's. Otherwise, Finley's fine-boned features didn't match much with Charlie's broader nose and wide jaw.

Big T had harassed Levi on the drive over, asking questions about his "mystery woman," but Levi had stuck to his story of how they were just friends. Big T didn't buy it for a minute, but Levi wasn't about to confide in anyone outside of what he'd already told Grizz.

Besides, he owed Grizz a picture of Finley, and Levi was still trying to figure out how to get that accomplished. Levi held the door open for Finley. Her dad was caught up in a conversation with Scrubs, and they seemed to be breaking down the game, play by play.

When Finley passed by Levi, she gave him a half smile, and he caught her scent of raspberry. He hated that for the next hour they'd be surrounded by a crowd of people in a loud pub. He wanted to talk to her, find out why she'd come to the game after all, if that meant things were okay between them. If things were okay with her dad.

Finley in her waitressing uniform was a beautiful sight, but out of it, she was something else. Her shorts were rather short, and the dark-yellow T-shirt she wore complemented her olive complexion. Her black hair was pulled into a high ponytail, showing off her silver hoops on her earlobes. Her strappy wedge sandals only made her long legs look longer, and he had to drag his gaze away so that her dad wouldn't catch him ogling.

The hostess led them to their reserved tables, and Levi sat across from Finley and her dad. It was probably just as well. If he'd been able to sit next to her, it would have been hard not to hold her hand, and he didn't know how her dad would react to that.

The waitress brought a round of drinks. "Welcome," she said. "Any appetizers?"

Big T ordered a couple of baskets of cheese fries. When the waitress left, everyone turned to their menus, talking about the game as they did so. Charlie Gray seemed to fit right in, throwing comments out left and right, not hesitant to share his opinion.

Finley didn't say much, just smiled and answered any questions sent her way.

Levi kept up his part of the conversation, but mostly he watched Finley. When the waitress returned to take their orders, Levi hadn't even read anything on the menu, at least nothing that he'd comprehended. Finley ordered some sort of salad, her dad ordered a French dip sandwich, and Levi chose a chicken sandwich. The other guys put in their orders, then as they waited for food, the conversation turned to discussion over brawls—who started them and who ended them—and by the time the conversation changed again, Levi was painted as some sort of hero, defending everyone's honor on the team.

Levi suspected that Scrubs and Big T were in on something together—maybe a game of "impress the woman's father on behalf of Levi." Whatever it was, it seemed to be working. Charlie Gray was all smiles.

Their food arrived, and although Levi was pretty much starving, his stomach was a knot of nerves. He'd never really cared to get on the good side of a woman's father before. He hadn't dated anyone seriously enough. With Finley, it was different.

"You any good at darts, Old Man Gray?" Big T asked. Charlie had already been dubbed with a nickname.

"I can hold my own," Charlie said with a grin.

Big T laughed. "Let's see what you can do, then."

The two men rose, and a couple of the others joined in. They headed to the other side of the pub, where some dart games were in progress. Scrubs and Nine were engrossed in a conversation with a couple of ladies at a nearby table. Levi could only guess how their nights would end up.

"So . . ." Finley began once they weren't surrounded by his teammates. "How long do we have to stay here? I thought we had a date. Unless *this* is what you had in mind."

Levi rose from his chair, walked around the table, and sat in the chair next to hers. Then he draped an arm across the back of her chair and leaned close. "This isn't what I had in mind, but you showed up with your dad. What else was I supposed to do?"

She turned her head to meet his gaze. "It was kind of a last-minute thing." She placed a hand on his leg, and his heart about leapt into his throat. "I wasn't planning on it either."

"Which?" he asked. "Coming to the game or bringing your dad?"

She smiled. "Both."

His heart stuttered. "What changed your mind?"

Finley didn't say anything for a second. "You. You've been genuine and honest, and I think you have a good heart."

He stared into the warmth of her brown eyes. "Well, thank you, Finley Gray."

Her cheeks dimpled, and he wondered how long he was going to have to wait to kiss her again. Levi slid his hand over her hand on his thigh and linked their fingers.

He leaned close again. "Do you think your dad would care if we left?"

She looked to where her dad was playing darts with the guys. "I think he's having the time of his life and won't care one bit. Besides, I want to see your place."

"*My* place?" Levi couldn't have been more surprised. "Are you hitting me up?"

She smiled. "I think I've got you almost figured out, Mr. Florida, but a man's home is a window to his soul."

He really didn't have an answer to that. His place was pretty bleak. She could make what she wanted of that, because tonight he was all about changing locations and taking Finley with him.

"Let's go." Levi released her hand so he could pull out his wallet. He placed a couple of hundred-dollar bills on the table.

Finley watched him with a smirk, then he grasped her hand again and led her toward the dart game. He wondered if she'd pull her hand away when they reached her dad, but she didn't.

"Hey, Dad," Finley said. "We're going to take off. Are you okay to stay here? You've got your car anyway."

Her dad turned. "Sure thing, honey." He kissed Finley's cheek, then shook Levi's hand. "Nice to meet you."

"Great to meet you too," Levi said. It was kind of a surreal moment, and he didn't miss the significance of it, at least for himself.

"Ready?" he asked Finley.

She squeezed his hand, and it made things happen in his chest. He didn't even care that his teammates could see him with Finley. They might razz him later, but he'd gladly take it. As they headed to the parking lot, Levi realized that he was in no hurry to get this night over with. Finley didn't protest about riding in his Bronco this time.

"I need to prepare you," Levi said as they pulled into his condo complex. "I was being honest when I said I don't have a couch."

"Why not?"

He cut her a glance as he parked the Bronco. "Never found the right one, I guess."

When they entered his apartment, Levi noticed the starkness of it as if he were new to the place. Compared to Finley's apartment, it looked like an empty warehouse.

"You said you didn't have a couch, but you don't have anything else either," Finley said, walking to the center of the room and stopping. "You weren't kidding about this place."

Granted, there were two folding chairs in the living room. "I wasn't kidding."

She glanced over at him. "Did you recently move in or something?"

"Four years ago."

Finley walked to the end of the room, then turned, her hands on her hips. "I'm going to build you a couch. You can choose the upholstery."

He gazed at her for a moment. Some tendrils of hair had come out of her ponytail, and her cheeks looked flushed. He didn't like her all the way across the room. "You really don't have to do that." He walked toward her, but she sidestepped him.

Heading into the kitchen, she said, "I'm glad you at least have a table."

Levi followed her into the kitchen and watched her inspect the table, then the two mismatched chairs.

"You could paint these," she said. "They'd look brand new."

He didn't answer, but leaned against the counter. He liked Finley at his place, even though she was inspecting it thoroughly.

She lifted her gaze to look at the kitchen walls, which were absolutely plain. "You could do with some paint as well. It's sort of a gray tinge right now—very . . ." She looked at him. "Boring."

He lifted his brows. "Boring? Is that the window to my soul you hoped to see?"

She didn't laugh. Instead, she moved closer to him, looking over the cupboards and counters. "You're not even close to boring, Levi Cox."

She stopped a few feet away from him and leaned against the counter. "Why do you live like this?"

Levi blinked. No one had ever asked him this kind of question so directly. Sure, any of his buddies who saw his place gave him a hard time.

"You mean, why do I live without all the fancy stuff?" he asked.

She folded her arms. "A guy who throws down a hundred-dollar bill to pay for a twenty-dollar plate isn't denying himself the fancy stuff. He's avoiding something."

Levi had no idea where she was going with this. "What am I avoiding?"

She merely looked at him. "You tell me."

He straightened from the counter and moved toward her. She watched him approach but didn't move as he stopped in front of her and placed his hands on the counter on either side of her. Her raspberry scent made her all the more kissable. "I could say the same thing about you."

Her brown eyes held his gaze. "What are you talking about?"

"You won't tell me why you really box," he said in a quiet voice. "Where all that energy comes from."

Her mouth twitched. "I guess we both have our secrets."

Levi scanned her face, from her brown eyes to her upturned chin. He lifted a hand and smoothed back an escaped tendril of her hair, then he let his fingers trail down her neck. "I, for one, like my gray walls. Remember, gray is my favorite color."

"I remember," she said, her voice soft.

He leaned a bit closer. Breathed in raspberries. Rested his hand on the curve between her neck and shoulder. Her skin was warm, and her pulse fluttered beneath his thumb.

"You need a couch at the very least," she said. "I mean, where do you sit and relax?"

"I don't."

Her dimples appeared. "You're kind of a stubborn man." She wasn't touching him, but his heart was racing anyway.

"I've been called worse." He slid his hand over her shoulder, then down her arm. When his fingers moved from the short sleeve of her shirt to her warm skin, goose bumps broke out on her arm.

Still, she didn't move. "So where do you want me to sit when I visit?" Her voice was light, coy.

He gazed into the warm brown of her eyes as he shifted his hand to her waist. He placed his other hand on her waist, then moved them lower, over her hips. With a single movement, he lifted her onto the counter.

"There's plenty of counter space," he said, stepping closer.

Finley laughed and wrapped her arms about his neck. "Terrible argument, Mr. Florida. I'm finding you a couch, and you're going to love it."

He couldn't help but smile. "You're kind of bossy."

"I think that's what it takes being around a hardheaded guy like you." She moved her fingers at the edge of his hair, drawing him closer.

"Thanks for coming to my game," he said.

Her smile was soft. "Thanks for inviting me."

"You're welcome," he whispered. Then he was done waiting. He kissed the edge of her mouth.

She seemed to sigh into him, and he pressed his mouth against hers fully.

Finley nestled her legs around his waist and drew him even closer as she kissed him back. Now he was the one with goose bumps. He didn't know what it was about this woman that drew him in so much, but when he kissed her, it was like his world was reduced to one thing—her.

"So is that a *yes* on the couch?" she asked, drawing away.

He slid his hands behind her back and kissed her again. "You can do whatever you want to my place."

Chapter 14

Finley decided that she rather liked kissing Levi while sitting on his counter, but a couch would be better. His kisses were plenty heated, yet she could tell he was holding back, which she was grateful for. Levi in small doses was overwhelming enough. And being at the pub with her dad and Levi's teammates had driven her crazy, since she'd much rather have him to herself.

Which only told her that her heart was getting involved with this man, probably too quickly. A week ago, she hadn't even known he existed, and now . . . he was kissing her quite thoroughly, and she was thinking all kinds of things that she shouldn't be thinking. Especially for a first date—or maybe it was a second?

Levi kissed her slowly, and her heart thumped like mad. Everywhere he touched her sent rivulets of heat through the rest of her body. His hands were splayed across her lower back, and the length of his body pressed against hers. He smelled of fresh shower and pine and maleness all in one.

"This isn't so bad, is it?" he whispered. "You look good on my counter."

Finley couldn't help but laugh. "I can honestly say I've never heard that line before."

His smile was brief before he kissed her forehead. "That's because it's not a line."

She ran her hands over his shoulders. She loved the way they were built, sturdy, muscled, yet warm and soft. "Okay, whatever. There are a few garage sales this weekend that I'm going to hit up."

"Mmm. Can we talk about that stuff later?" he asked, kissing her temple, then her neck just below her jaw, then moving lower.

Finley exhaled as her skin tingled with his trail of kisses. She placed her hands on his chest to put the smallest bit of space between them, although feeling his heart thump only made her pulse increase a notch. "I think we should plan now because you probably have a game," she said, her voice coming out breathless. "And I'm working too. Garage sales are best first thing Saturday mornings."

Levi pressed a kiss on her collarbone, then lifted his head. "I'll be in Belltown Friday night. I fly back Saturday morning. My game's Saturday night, so I have to be at the field by two."

"Belltown?" she said. "That's your college, right?"

"Yeah," he said, moving his hands to her waist. "It's Belltown Days, and it's kind of a big deal. They have a parade float for the Six Pack. Fireworks, the whole bit. My brother will be there too."

"That's right," she said. "You told me he's at Belltown University. Does he have a couch in *his* apartment?"

Levi smirked. "He does. Remember, we're pretty much opposites."

"He doesn't play baseball and start brawls?"

"Not even close," Levi said. "He's the smart kid in the family. I have to do the dirty work."

She smiled, and Levi's gaze searched hers. Then he leaned forward again, and his pine scent was filling her own senses. His warm lips touched hers, and she closed her eyes.

Kissing Levi was like being in that half-awake state between dreaming and waking up. She rested her hands on his biceps. Levi lifted his hands and cradled her face.

"You should come," he said quietly.

She blinked. "What?"

His thumbs brushed across her jaw. "Big Dawg is picking up Grizz and me in his private jet tomorrow afternoon. You can be my date, and I'll, you know, show you around Belltown."

Finley swallowed. Did he know what he was asking? This was boyfriend-girlfriend stuff.

His hands moved to her shoulders. "What?"

"I don't want to get in the middle of all that," she said. "And a private jet? I thought Big Dawg was a centerfielder."

Levi grinned. "He is. His real money comes from his dad—Texas millionaire stuff."

"I'm on shift."

Levi studied her, his gaze penetrating, making it hard for Finley to turn him down. "Get the night off."

"It's a Friday night," she continued. "You know, a weekend, so super busy."

"I know," he whispered, leaning down again and pressing a brief kiss on her mouth. "Think about it. Talk to your boss. We fly out at one."

Finley exhaled. "I can't. I'm sorry." She was flattered by the invitation in the first place. It showed that Levi wasn't hooking up with her. It showed that he liked her beyond superficial stuff.

"Well, you have my number if you change your mind," he said.

"Yeah, I do," she said. "And I think you'd better take me home now, Mr. Florida."

"So soon?"

"I have a double shift tomorrow," she said, "and I have to plan out my garage-sale route for Saturday morning. This place needs a lot of work."

"So . . . if I had a couch, you'd stay longer?" he asked.

"Too late to find out," she said, smiling. She pushed on his chest, then slid off the counter.

Levi captured her hand, but she continued toward the door, pulling him with her.

"Okay, okay," he said. "We're leaving, I guess."

They held hands as they walked to his Bronco, and he stole another kiss before she climbed into the passenger seat.

Her pulse fluttered as she watched him walk around the Bronco. The more she was with Levi, the more she liked him. She hadn't known what to think when she walked into Levi's almost empty apartment. It had a barren feel to it, as if he was afraid to put down roots. Or maybe he didn't know how since he'd never had roots. Finley couldn't imagine what it might be like to live in foster care. Never having something that belonged to you. Never having a true home to call yours.

When he climbed into the Bronco, she said, "I've figured you out."

Levi snapped his gaze to hers. "Really," he deadpanned.

"Yes, really." She glanced out the window as he drove, and the buildings sped by. "You won't furnish your place because you never had anything of your own as a kid. You never had a real home. So it's easier to not settle in. To not get attached to anything."

He was silent for so long that Finley wondered if she'd offended him.

"That makes a twisted sort of sense," he said finally. "But

the truth is, I don't really care about stuff like furniture or decorations."

"That's part of it," she said in a quiet voice. "You don't *let* yourself care."

When he pulled up to her apartment building, he put the Bronco into park and turned off the ignition.

"You don't have to walk me up," she said. "I'll be fine."

"I'm walking you up," he said, opening his door. "I won't come in if you don't want me to."

"Now who's being stubborn?"

Levi smiled, but his gaze was serious.

She waited for him to come around and open her door. Then he held out his hand, and she set hers in his.

When they reached her apartment door, Levi said, "So do you think your dad likes me now?"

Finley held up her phone. "He's sent several texts about playing darts with your teammates. I think that translates into a great night for him, which could also translate into him liking you."

Levi took her phone and glanced through her dad's texts. He smiled. "Nice logic."

When he handed her phone back, he moved closer, his dark-green eyes on her. "Call me tomorrow and tell me what you've decided about Belltown."

"I already decided," she said, although her voice sounded hesitant to her own ears.

He leaned down and kissed her cheek, lingering. "Still call me."

Then he stepped away, and she wished he'd give her a real kiss. But she knew it would be almost impossible to send him away again. She turned toward her door and opened it. Then she went into her apartment and locked the door behind her.

She made her way in the dark to the front window, where she had a view of the street.

She watched Levi get into the Bronco and drive away. Her heart pinged, and she already missed him. Leaning her forehead against the window, she closed her eyes. Things were moving fast. And she didn't know how she felt about that. On one hand, she really liked Levi, and on the other hand, she knew her heart was in real danger of being broken. The more she allowed herself to like Levi Cox, the more vulnerable she'd become.

He'd told her a lot about his past, but she knew there were more things, deeper things he probably never talked about. Seeing his barren apartment tonight had made it hard to ignore. She thought of the young boy that he'd once been, moving from one foster home to another. And her heart cracked thinking of how scared he must have been. And how much responsibility and worry he'd taken on at such a young age as he tried to be a good older brother to Rhett.

Finley blew out a breath. And now Levi had asked her to go to Belltown with him. They'd be surrounded by the Six Pack, Levi's closest friends, and she'd meet his brother. Her mind spun thinking about it all.

Was this something she could ask her dad for advice on?

No, because she'd already turned Levi down. So it wasn't even a concern. Right?

Or maybe Mark would be cool and let her only do the morning shift tomorrow. Maybe if someone covered for her Friday night, she could work a double on Sunday. Maybe . . .

Sometimes Finley wished she had a good girlfriend, someone she could ask advice from. But she'd never really had other female friends. The closest she got to women was when she was facing one in a boxing ring. And any advice from Jess or one of the other waitresses at the pub would be useless.

Finley settled on one of her couches, sitting in the dark, and scrolled through her dad's texts. *I beat Big T in our dart game. Three games out of five.* About twenty minutes later, he'd sent: *Just beat Scrubs. He's paying for dessert.*

Finley smiled, then read the next text. *Turns out the Ice plays in town Saturday night, and they all want a rematch. Same pub.*

She texted her dad back. *Sounds fun. I'll be working, but I can see if Levi can get you tickets again.*

Her dad wrote back almost immediately. *Scrubs says he'll get me covered.*

Wow. She wondered if Levi's teammates thought she and Levi were more serious than they were. Or was Scrubs that nice of a guy and didn't mind hanging out with a fifty-year-old guy?

The question about Belltown still burned in her mind, and she knew it would be hard to get to sleep tonight. As if Levi knew she was thinking about him, he texted her. *I think you're right. I need a couch.*

She laughed. *I knew you'd come around.*

Have you changed your mind yet about Belltown? he wrote.

Finley debated whether to tell him that she was thinking of talking to Mark in the morning. Feel things out. But she didn't want to give Levi hope when there might be none. *I have a couch to find.*

Believe me, I'm in no hurry, he texted. *It's been four years. Another week won't matter. Besides, you haven't lived until you've had a donut from Sinclairs. Assuming you're a donut person.*

I like donuts, she wrote. *Maybe you can bring me one back.*

No. Not the same, he wrote. *You have to eat them fresh, or it doesn't count.*

Finley smiled. *If you ever get cut from the Minnesota Ice, you can go into sales, Mr. Florida.*

His reply came quick. *I'm having a hard time convincing you.*

Levi Cox could be persistent when he wanted to. Probably how he kept rising in the baseball ranks. *Good night, Levi. Have a safe trip.*

Good night, Finley.

She pressed the phone against her chest and closed her eyes. Her dreams about Levi would be sweet tonight.

CHAPTER 15

"Y'ALL WANT SOMETHING to drink?" Big Dawg asked, leading Levi into the main cabin of his private jet. "Refueling will only take about twenty."

"Steal!" Grizz said, rising from his luxury lounge chair. "It's been too long."

Levi laughed. "Not long enough." He slapped Grizz's shoulder.

Grizz chuckled. "Can you believe the getup Big Dawg's wearing?"

Levi smirked. "Not surprised. I see a guy wearing yellow shoes and a yellow baseball cap, and I know it's gotta be Cole Hunter."

"Hey, these are limited edition," Big Dawg said, turning the brim of his hat to the back of his head. "I also got something special for the parade."

Big Dawg sauntered over to a table and picked up a shoe box. He opened it, and Levi laughed. "Flag-printed shoes? You're kidding me."

Grizz hooted. "The parade queens won't be able to keep their eyes off you, or stop laughing. One of the two."

"Rumor has it that you're wearing a dress to the parade," Dawg said. "Something to do with a bet you lost against Steal."

Grizz shut up.

Big Dawg grinned. "Well, I'm used to the attention from the ladies. And my shoes will give them an extra reason to love me. Patriotic gestures go straight to the heart."

Grizz scoffed and retook his seat.

Levi sat across from Grizz on the plush leather recliner. He'd been in Big Dawg's jet more than once, and he never failed to appreciate it. Made flying first class on a commercial liner feel like riding on a cargo plane.

"Thanks for picking me up," Levi said.

Big Dawg opened the mini-fridge and pulled out a couple of water bottles. "No problem. I was worried one of you would bail on me, so this ensures that y'all show up. Plus with Grizz playing in South Dakota last night, you were on the way."

"I'll take one of those," Levi said, and Dawg tossed the water bottle.

Levi caught it, then downed half of the water.

Both Dawg and Grizz had played last night and won their games, so they started talking about some plays. Levi listened, but his mind was mostly elsewhere. On Finley, to be exact. He'd texted her before leaving for the airport, and she hadn't responded yet. He knew she didn't text much during her shift. Still, he wished he'd hear from her before he'd have to turn off his phone.

"You're in outer space," Grizz said, cutting into his thoughts.

Levi looked over at Grizz, hoping the guy wouldn't bring up Finley. He was the only one of the Six Pack who knew he was dating, and Levi didn't want to spend the next eighteen hours fielding questions or fending off jokes.

Grizz folded his arms. "Will Rhett be hanging with us?"

"He better be," Levi said. "He's been dating some woman, so I'd better be meeting her too."

Dawg laughed. "I'm sure Rhett loves how you act like his dad."

Levi threw a glare at Dawg, and Grizz said, "You know you can't throw down on Levi's family, unless you want a black eye."

"Fine." Dawg raised his hands as if he were completely innocent. "I'm backing off now. But I agree with Grizz. You're like in outer space right now."

Levi rubbed the back of his neck. "I'm here."

Dawg scoffed, and Grizz smirked.

Levi's phone rang, and he pulled it from his pocket. His breath stalled when he saw Finley's name. He had hoped to hear from her, but he hadn't expected her to call. Did he even want to answer with Grizz and Dawg sitting three feet away from him?

But maybe it was important, some sort of emergency, or . . .

"Hi," he answered.

"Hi, oh, um, I didn't realize it was twelve thirty," she said, sounding like she was out of breath or nervous or something. "It's later than I thought. You're probably already at the airport."

"Just got on the plane," he said, trying to analyze her tone of voice. He glanced at Grizz and Dawg. They were both solely focused on him. Great.

"Oh, okay," Finley said. "Well, have a good flight."

She did sound nervous. What was going on? Levi stood and paced away from his audience, but he very well knew they could hear every single word. "Did you get work off?"

The hesitation came through the phone. "Well, Mark said he could swing it if I took tonight off. I'd have to work a double on Sunday. But you're already on the plane, and I could use the extra time to get some upholstery fabric—"

"Hang on, okay?" He put the phone to his chest and looked at Big Dawg. "Can we wait about thirty minutes for another person?"

"*Person*?" Big Dawg asked.

Grizz kicked Dawg's foot. "Yes, we can," Grizz said.

Dawg cut his gaze to Grizz, and Grizz raised his brows. "Yes. We. Can," Grizz repeated.

Dawg's eyes widened. "Oh. *That* kind of person." He looked over at Levi with a grin. "Sure thing. When will she be here?"

Levi turned away from the gawkers and told Finley, "We can wait."

"Tell her the TSA agent will meet her at security and get her through," Dawg said. "I'll call them right now."

"Did you hear that?" Levi asked.

"Yeah, but are you sure?" Finley asked. "I mean—"

"I'm sure," he said.

"We're sure!" Dawg called out.

Grizz laughed.

Levi hung up with Finley, his heart soaring. She was coming. And he couldn't believe how happy that made him.

He turned to face his friends. Both Grizz and Big Dawg were grinning.

Dawg held up his phone. "Got TSA on right now. What's her name?"

"Finley Gray."

Dawg said a few things into his phone, then hung up and folded his arms. "Why is this the first I have heard of Miss Finley Gray?"

Levi exhaled, then took his seat. Before he could answer,

Grizz jumped in. "Because they only met last week. And apparently Levi's already whipped."

Levi shifted his gaze to Grizz, hoping that he could read minds and would keep his mouth shut.

But Grizz couldn't read minds. Either that, or he didn't care about Levi's privacy.

"He met her at a pub where she works as a waitress," Grizz continued, smiling at Big Dawg. "And get this, she's a boxer."

Dawg laughed. "Are y'all serious? I can't wait to meet this little darlin'. Or is 'little' the wrong word?"

Levi felt his face heat. "She's a perfectly normal size."

"A perfectly normal woman who likes to punch people in the face?" Dawg said, laughter still in his voice.

"It's a sport," Levi said. "And don't call her *darlin'*."

Grizz chuckled. "Good luck with that. I think Big Dawg would call a door *darlin'* if he bumped into it."

Dawg raised both his hands. "All right. All right. Don't get all worked up, man. Just having some fun." He leaned back in his chair, stretched out his legs, and crossed his ankles. "I never thought I'd see the day when Levi Cox got all flustered over a lady. It's a good day, in my humble Texan opinion."

Levi shook his head and gazed out the miniature window.

"How long have you known about this?" Dawg asked Grizz in a conspiratorial whisper that was loud and clear.

"Not long," Grizz answered. "Like I said, he met her last week. Anything else you want to know, Steal will have to tell you. I'm not going to get on his bad side."

Dawg looked pointedly at Levi, who scowled.

"You know I'm gonna be cool," Dawg said. "Nothing embarrassing will come from my mouth. Cross my Texan heart."

Levi exhaled. "Fine. Like Grizz said, I met Finley at a pub

last week—where she works. I saw a poster about her boxing match, so I went to watch later that night." He shrugged. "We've hung out a couple of times. Nothing major, and nothing that's any of your business."

Dawg waggled his brows. "So . . . you kissed her."

Levi didn't answer.

"You're right," Grizz said. "Levi can blush."

Both Grizz and Dawg laughed.

"Okay, look," Levi cut in. "I like her. And I think she likes me. Her dad's super protective of her and doesn't love the idea of his daughter dating a professional athlete, because some of us have crappy reputations."

Both Dawg and Grizz put on innocent-as-a-baby expressions.

"She brought her dad to the game last night," Levi continued. "And he seems pretty cool with stuff now. But things are still new with Finley, so you both need to know that payback's a b—"

"We get it," Dawg said with a laugh. "Besides, I like her already, and if anyone can put up with Levi Cox, it's a boxer chick."

When Finley texted *I'm through security*, Levi rose to his feet. He felt Grizz and Dawg's gaze on him as he went to the door to wait for her. Soon Levi saw her come out of an airport door, a TSA employee walking with her. Finley carried a backpack slung over one shoulder. She was wearing a blue sundress, and her hair was down, waving over her shoulders. He hadn't seen her look so dressed up before.

It took Levi a second to realize he meant to meet her at the bottom of the steps. He headed down them and reached the tarmac as she reached the stairs.

"She's set to go," the TSA guy told Levi, as if Levi were the owner of the jet.

"Thanks," Levi told him, and he handed over a ten-dollar bill. He didn't know the protocol, but he might as well cover all the bases. He watched the TSA guy walk away, then he turned to Finley. The warm breeze stirred her hair, and she had some sort of shiny lip gloss on.

"I like your dress," he said in a quiet voice.

Her cheeks dimpled. "I thought I'd have to go a little fancy for a private jet."

He stepped closer and slipped his hands around her waist. She moved easily into his arms, and he pulled her into an embrace. Not a long one, because he was pretty sure Big Dawg and Grizz were watching out the windows.

"I'm glad you changed your mind," he whispered against her ear.

"I'm glad you're glad." Her fingers were warm against his neck.

He smiled and breathed in her raspberry scent. "I need to warn you about my friends. Grizz and Big Dawg sometimes revert to their ten-year-old selves."

She drew away, keeping her arms looped about his neck. "You forget where I work."

"Right . . ." He wanted to kiss her, but it wouldn't be a short kiss. So he slid the backpack from her shoulder, grabbed her hand, and led her up the stairs to face whatever might come.

Chapter 16

Finley tried not to gawk at the interior of the private jet, but the thing was gorgeous, from the plush carpet to the leather furniture and wood accents, to the soft lighting. "Wow," she said under her breath, and Levi squeezed her hand.

Then she looked over at the two guys who'd risen from their seats.

She might have googled the Six Pack a time or two, so she knew immediately which one was Grizz—full beard and all. His beard did nothing to hide his attractiveness. Cole Hunter, a.k.a. Big Dawg, was a different species altogether. Where Grizz was more the rugged, outdoor type of guy, Big Dawg was all polish and magazine gorgeous.

"Finley, this is Cole Hunter and David McCarthy," Levi said.

"Hello, sunshine," Cole said, stepping forward and holding out his hand.

Finley placed her hand in his, and she felt miniature compared to the size of his palm.

"So glad y'all could make it," he continued, his smile as white as a toothpaste commercial.

"Thanks for waiting," Finley said, trying to comprehend that not only was she dating Levi Cox, but now she was hanging out with his Major League baseball friends. In a private jet.

She turned to David—Grizz—and shook his hand too. There was something comfortable about him, totally unpretentious. She could imagine him tossing a ball to a kid at a park just as much as she could imagine him staring down Levi as he'd done the other night.

"Nice to meet you," Grizz said.

"I'll be right back, darlin'," Cole said. "I mean, *sunshine*. I need to tell the captain we're ready." He winked at Finley, then moved past her to go to the cockpit.

There had to be a story behind Cole's use of endearments, or was it the Texan in him?

Levi motioned to one of the recliners. "Have a seat. Do you want something to drink? Dawg has the fridge stocked with pretty much anything you could want."

"Water's fine," she said, seeing the other water bottles around.

Levi crossed to a built-in refrigerator and pulled out a water bottle, then handed it to her.

"Thanks," she said, twisting off the cap and taking a sip. It was ice cold and exactly what she needed. She hadn't been sure what Levi's reaction would be if she showed up wearing a dress, but when she'd seen the appreciation in his eyes, it had made her glad of her decision. And when he'd hugged her so sweetly, she was pretty sure she was about to melt on the spot.

Finley took another sip of the cold water. Then she put the water bottle in the cupholder attached to her comfy recliner. She glanced over at Grizz, who'd picked up a magazine on polar bears that she doubted he had any interest in. But he seemed to be politely giving her and Levi their space.

Levi sat on her left and clipped on his seatbelt.

So Finley did likewise.

"Have you been thinking about colors?" she asked quietly.

Levi turned his head. "Colors?"

"You know, for your couch."

Grizz arched an eyebrow and flipped a page on his magazine.

"No..." Levi said in a low voice, "I've just been thinking about you."

Warmth jolted through Finley. Despite the glamour of Cole Hunter and the handsome ruggedness of Grizz, it was Levi's dark-green eyes that drew her in. He hadn't shaved today, and she had the sudden desire to lean toward him and run her fingers over the stubble on his jaw.

"You're getting a couch for Levi?" Cole said, coming back into the cabin. He sat across from Finley and crossed his legs, his blue-green eyes bright with interest. Or was it amusement?

"Sort of." Finley felt the tension coming from Levi. But these were his best friends, right? "I refinish furniture and reupholster couches and chairs. Frames usually last a lot longer than cushions and fabric."

Cole nodded, looking impressed. "My best friend in high school did that with his mom. It was pretty cool."

The plane began to move, and Cole clipped on his seatbelt. "You too, Grizz," he said without looking over.

Grizz complied and buckled his seatbelt, then he returned to his magazine.

"So how did you talk Steal into getting a couch?" Cole continued. "He's never listened to my suggestions."

Next to her, Levi scoffed, but he didn't say anything. The jet accelerated, and Finley glanced out the window, then refocused on Cole.

"Maybe he wasn't ready when you suggested it."

Cole's brows shot up, and he smiled. "And he's ready now?"

Finley shrugged and matched Cole's smile.

The jet rose into the air. Finley decided it would be a good time to steer the conversation away from Levi. She could feel him glowering without even looking at him. "This jet is amazing," Finley told Cole.

He nodded. "Yeah, it's something. Want the grand tour?"

"Sure," Finley said, glancing over at Levi.

"Go ahead, I've seen it," he said.

So Finley unsnapped her seatbelt and stood.

"We'll start at the back," Cole said.

They walked past a kitchenette and another lounge area.

Cole opened a door and motioned for her to go inside.

Finley stepped past him and walked into a room. The place was a full bedroom—bed, nightstand, dresser, the works. "There's a bed in here?"

"Makes it convenient when I have to fly across the country in the middle of the night," Cole said, leaning against the doorway and watching her move about the room.

With the door shut, it would feel like a regular hotel room. A really nice one. Amazing. She turned to face Cole. "This is nicer than most people's houses."

Cole nodded. "Yeah, especially Steal's. You should have seen his college apartment. Slept on a mattress on a floor. Didn't even buy a bed frame. He really was broke back then, but now? He can dish out something."

"I can hear you," Levi called from the other room.

Cole grinned, then lowered his voice. "Steal's like a hoarder. Of money. You know those stories about people who came through a war and how they collect things in Mason jars. Like buttons and bits of soap?"

"I don't own a single Mason jar," Levi said.

Cole laughed and led Finley out of the room. He stopped at a large kitchenette. "This here's the kitchen. Well-stocked, so if y'all get hungry, I can whip up something."

Grizz chuckled from where he was sitting. "The day I see Big Dawg cook for another person is the day I start pitching."

"There's plenty of catchers who can pitch," Cole shot back. He opened a cupboard. "See, SpaghettiOs. Even I can warm those up."

"Thanks," Finley said, holding back a laugh. "I'm not hungry."

"Okay, but if you want SpaghettiOs, sunshine, I'm your guy," Cole said.

Although everything that Cole Hunter said to her could be deemed flirtatious, Finley sensed it was part of who he was. If she were eighty years old and had to board his jet pushing a walker, she believed he'd treat her the same way.

Finley smiled. "I'll let you know, Big Dawg."

He winked at her.

She retook her seat by Levi. Grizz returned to his intense study of the polar bear magazine, and Cole put on headphones, then connected them to an iPad.

"Are you regretting your decision yet?" Levi said in a quiet tone.

Finley turned her head to meet his dark-green gaze. She was surprised to see that his expression was somber, that he was truly thinking she might regret coming. "No," she said, reaching over to pat his hand. "Are you?"

"Never."

When he said things like that, it was hard to keep him at a distance. But they were surrounded by his friends.

Before she could withdraw her hand, Levi grasped it and

linked their fingers. Her skin tingled as he rubbed his thumb over the back of her hand.

"How long's the flight?" she asked.

"A couple of hours," Levi said.

"Just under three," Grizz commented, flipping another magazine page.

Levi shook his head. "Like I said, a couple of hours."

"Good." Finley pulled out her phone and opened to the pictures she'd screenshotted from Pinterest. "We can choose colors, then I can email in the order when we land. Sal can have the upholstery fabric ready by tomorrow if I get it in soon enough."

"Like I said, I'm not in any hurry."

"I know."

"And you haven't even found a couch yet."

"I know."

Levi smiled, and she smiled back. She was one hundred percent certain if they weren't with Grizz and Cole, Levi would have kissed her.

Well, she could wait. Holding his hand was enough for now, and more than she'd expected. Yeah, he'd invited her on this trip, and she'd changed things around to come, but she hadn't known Levi would be this invested in her. Holding her hand in front of friends, saying sweet things knowing that they could overhear.

"Okay, show me your ideas," Levi said.

Grizz chuckled and flipped another magazine page. Were polar bears funny?

Finley showed Levi the pictures on her phone, colors ranging from blues to muted yellows.

"No yellow or orange or red," Levi said. "And turquoise is also out."

That canceled about seventy percent of her photos. "So . . . brown?"

"Gray or black would be fine too," Levi said.

"Right . . . gray." Finley exhaled. "What about blue?"

"Dark blue."

"You've got your work cut out for you, sunshine," Cole said, apparently not engrossed in his iPad after all.

Finley smirked and looked up at Levi. His gaze was trained on her, not on the pictures on her phone. Her pulse went up a notch. She drank more of her water, which was less cold now. She finished it off, then said, "I guess I'll surprise you then."

"No flowers. Promise."

She laughed. "No floral print, I promise."

Levi was still staring at her like he was about to pull her onto his lap and kiss her. She really needed some distance, because she was finding she wouldn't mind that course of action. "I'm going to get more water." She pulled her hand from Levi's and stood.

Levi stood as well. "I can get it," he said.

Cole rose to his feet, his iPad forgotten. "I can get you water."

Finley looked from Cole to Levi. "Really, guys, I can get my own water." She lightly shoved Levi's chest so that he would sit down again. She walked past Cole, who grinned.

"I agree, she can get her own water," Grizz chipped in, his tone on the edge of laughter.

Finley was probably blushing ten shades of red thanks to all this attention.

It wasn't every day she had the full attention of three men. She grabbed the water bottle and went back to her seat. Grizz had returned to his polar bear magazine, and Cole had put his earbuds back in. Finley wasn't fooled though.

"Are the next eighteen hours going to be like this?" she asked Levi.

"It might get worse," Levi said. "You've only met half of us."

Chapter 17

"Can I drive?" Levi asked the red-faced man with a giant mustache, who'd introduced himself as Red. Fitting.

"Nope, the Six Pack are all supposed to be *on* the float," Red said, hooking his thumbs into his belt loops. "Waving at the crowd and tossing candy to the kids. The driving is my job."

Levi cast another glance at the baby-blue convertible Cadillac. Not only was the car beautiful, but he'd be able to take advantage of the air conditioning. Apparently Belltown was in a heat wave, and the five o'clock parade start time meant that the heat and humidity would be at its worst. And the Six Pack were all wearing full Belltown University baseball uniforms.

And Grizz, true to his word, having lost his bet against Levi, had some sort of sarong over his uniform. Levi wasn't exactly sure if that should count as a dress, but he'd decided to let it go.

"What took you so long?" a familiar voice said.

Levi turned to see his brother, Rhett. Although he'd changed from boy to man a couple of years ago, Levi still saw him as a kid. Rhett had bleached his hair, and he'd gotten a tan over the summer. His brown eyes were from whoever was his dad. Rhett was also holding hands with a red-haired woman.

"I would have been here last weekend," Levi said.

Rhett laughed. "I know—and then you dropped off the planet. I thought maybe you'd decided not to come to Belltown for the parade."

"As if Skeeter would have let me get out of it." Belltown was Skeeter's hometown. Although he currently lived in Ohio and played for the Columbus Black Racers, he kept the Six Pack involved with Belltown as much as possible.

"Where is Skeet?" Rhett asked. "Did he make it?"

"He did," Levi said. "His team plays tonight, but his coach let him come since he wasn't in the pitching rotation. Everyone was at the barbeque food truck last I saw them." Along with Finley. He couldn't see her now either.

"So are you going to introduce me?" Levi prompted, his gaze moving to the woman with Rhett.

"Oh yeah," Rhett said. "Erin, this is my brother, Levi."

Levi shook her hand, and he liked that her grip was confident. "Where are you from?"

"Ah, here we go," Rhett said, rolling his eyes.

Erin only smiled, which made her blue eyes light up. "You guys remind me of my brothers."

"So we're awesome?" Rhett prompted.

Erin laughed, and Levi watched his brother grin. Levi had never seen his brother act so . . . happy. Carefree? Something.

"I'm from Belltown," Erin said. "It's pretty cool to meet a member of the Six Pack. You guys are legends."

Rhett groaned. "Please don't tell me you're dating me to get to my brother."

Erin elbowed him. "Your brother's like ten years older than you."

"Four."

"Oh, really?" She smiled. "That totally changes things up then."

Rhett grabbed her in a bear hug, and Erin laughed.

It did Levi's heart good to see his brother like this. Maybe Levi shouldn't have stressed so much when Rhett said he was dating.

"So who did you want me to meet?" Rhett said, releasing Erin but keeping an arm about her waist.

Both Rhett and Erin looked at Levi expectantly.

Levi rubbed the back of his neck. "Uh, she's here somewhere."

Then he caught a glimpse of her blue dress. Over by the craft booths. Finley was with another Belltown native, Harlow Ember, who'd gone to college with the Six Pack. Harlow now reported for the local newspaper, frequently writing about the Six Pack and their various Major League successes.

"Come on," Levi said. "Finley's over here."

"Finley?" Rhett said.

"Finley Gray," Levi clarified. His heart thudded as he walked with his brother and Erin over to the craft booths.

He'd just met the woman Rhett was dating, but this was different. He'd never introduced anyone to his brother, or to the Six Pack, for that matter.

Harlow saw him first. Her straight blond hair was shorter than he remembered it, and it made her look all grown up. "Steal!" she said, then hugged him.

"What are you up to, Ember?" he asked.

She drew away. "Same old stuff. But it sounds like you're finally getting some furniture."

Levi's gaze cut to Finley, whose eyes flashed with

laughter. He might as well own it, because there were no secrets in Belltown, or among the Six Pack, it seemed.

"Yep," he said, then changed the subject. "You know my brother, Rhett."

"I see him once in a while," Harlow said, giving him a wave.

"Hey," Rhett said, then he introduced Erin.

Finley moved to Levi's side. "And this is Finley," he told his brother.

Rhett smiled and shook her hand. "Nice to meet you. Where are you from?"

"Whatever, bro," Levi said.

Rhett laughed. "What? It's just a question."

A voice blared on a loudspeaker, announcing that the parade floats were about to move out. Someone shouted his name, and Levi looked to see Rabbit waving wildly at him.

"Looks like the parade is starting," Levi said, grasping Finley's hand and pulling her with him.

"We'll take pictures," Rhett called after him. "For your posterity."

"Wait, where are we going?" Finley asked as she walked with him.

"We have to get on the float," he said.

Finley tugged him to a stop. "Um, *you* have to get on the float. Not me."

He looked down at her. Her skin glowed with the humidity. "You're invited too. Remember, you're with me?"

Her cheeks dimpled, but she wouldn't budge. "I'll hang out with your brother. Take pictures of you and your cute uniform."

"You think I'm cute?" he asked, stepping closer.

She took a step back. "You know you're cute, Mr. Florida.

But I was talking about the uniform." She pulled her hand from his. "See you after the parade."

Levi frowned. "You're really going to ditch me?"

Her smile expanded, and her brown eyes sparked. "Bye, Levi."

He watched her walk back toward his brother, where he stood with Erin and Harlow. That blue dress really looked good on her.

"Steal!" Rabbit called. "We're pulling out!"

"Coming!" He jogged toward the float. The thing was already moving.

Rabbit laughed as Levi scrambled up onto the back of the float.

"Last but not least," Skeeter said. He wore his ball cap backwards like usual, his blue eyes filled with humor. "I hear she's a boxer."

"Among other things." Levi followed Skeeter's gaze to see Finley standing by his brother. Rhett was laughing about something. Maybe it hadn't been a good idea to introduce them quite yet. Now they'd have a lot of time together during the parade, and who knew what Rhett would tell her.

"What else?" Skeeter asked.

When Levi didn't reply, Skeet continued, "I could always ask the others."

Axel Diaz joined them, a knowing look in his brown eyes. He currently played shortstop for the Seattle Sharks, and his record at stealing bases almost rivaled Levi's. "I hear she rebuilds furniture," he supplied.

"Really." Skeeter folded his arms. "That's cool." He eyed Levi. "You gonna get a couch?"

Axel burst out laughing. "He is. How'd you guess?"

"Oh, I don't know," Skeet said, his grin almost wider than

his face. "Maybe because last time I was at his place in the Mini Apple, I had to sit on a freaking lawn chair."

"You guys are both idiots," Levi said. "And it was a padded folding chair, not a lawn chair."

This only made Axel laugh harder.

Levi shook his head. Maybe he'd stand on the other side of the float and toss candy to the kids. Although he suspected it wouldn't be much better, not with Grizz and Dawg there. It seemed they hadn't kept their mouths shut about a thing.

He looked over at Grizz; the guy had taken off his sarong-slash-dress. "Hey, where's your skirt?"

Grizz shrugged. "I wore it as promised, and then I took it off. You never said how long I had to wear it."

Levi shook his head, then he snatched up one of the candy bags full of salt-water taffy and Tootsie Rolls.

The parade seemed to drag on, both because the float only moved about three miles an hour and because Levi was anxious to get back to Finley. Maybe he could steal her away from everyone for a while, then later they'd catch the fireworks.

"Y'all are coming to the Little League banquet after the parade, right?" Dawg said. "Rabbit, did you send the info to everyone?"

"Not yet," Rabbit said. "Doing it now."

Dawg laughed. "Better late than never, I guess."

Cell phones started to ping as the texts transferred.

"You don't have to stay for the whole thing," Skeeter said, lifting up his ball cap and scratching at his light-brown hair. "Just come to the picture booth at the beginning, then when the kids get through, we can leave."

"Some of us might have made other plans," Levi said. As soon as the words left his mouth, he realized his mistake.

Dawg hooted. "Is that right, Steal?"

"My mom's on the committee," Skeeter cut in. "So no one gets to ditch."

Everyone looked at Skeeter.

"What?" Skeet raised his hands. "You don't think I'd commit us to any old Little League photo booth."

Skeeter's mom had been like a mom to all of them in college. Sally, or Mamma Sal, as they called her, was a sweetheart through and through. She'd been the one to give Levi advice about getting Rhett to attend college at Belltown. She'd also talked Levi out of one of his darker days when frustrations with life and baseball had been overwhelming.

It looked like they'd all be going to the photo op after the parade.

About three spots behind them, a marching band began to play. Dawg started dancing to the rhythm, and the crowd cheered. Levi had to laugh. Dawg had the signature moves and never let an opportunity pass to show them off.

The band's song turned from a patriotic number to Belltown University's school song as a huge guy dressed as a lumberjack jogged along the parade route.

Many in the crowd began singing along to the school song, encouraged by the presence of the Lumberjack Mascot.

"Hail to Belltown, hail to thee,
Proud and tall among the trees."

The Six Pack on the float joined in, draping their arms over each other's shoulders as they sang. Dawg pulled Levi into the group.

"Away we heave, away we hoe,
We see and saw and down they go,
Proud and mighty, strong and true."

The crowd sang back to the Six Pack: "The Lumberjacks are coming through!"

It was moments like this that Levi appreciated feeling a

part of something bigger than himself, something that connected him to roots. He'd never had a family, except for his brother, and standing on the float, singing with the best group of friends that a guy could ever hope to have, made him feel connected. They were his family.

The lumberjack character jogged alongside their float, pointing his axe at the baseball players. Dawg decided that meant singing even louder.

"Belltown! Belltown!
Ever grateful, ever there.
We're Lumberjacks, the bold who dare!"

Levi laughed at the spectacle they must be making.

The song came to an end as the entire crowd shouted in thunderous unison, "Ohhhh, Timberrrrrrrr!"

Chapter 18

"Let's get out of here," Levi told Finley, leaning close so that only she could hear.

"Why?" Finley said. "The fireworks just started." Overhead, the sky crackled with light and sound as she and Levi sat among the Six Pack. Levi's brother and his girlfriend sat nearby as well, along with Mamma Sal, her daughter, Rachel, and Harlow Ember, including a few others Finley had been introduced to. Spread across the baseball field were groups of families and teenagers sitting on blankets or the grass. Some had brought camping chairs.

Levi linked his fingers with hers, and predictably, warmth shot through her. They'd been together most of the day, but their touching had been restricted to hand holding. Maybe Levi was ready for something more. The thought of kissing him again made the warmth boil over and spread to other parts of her body.

"Please." His voice was a husky whisper.

Finley sort of liked how he was basically begging.

"Okay," she said. "But only because you said *please*."

"I guess I found out your magic password," he said.

Finley laughed, and a couple of heads turned in their direction. Levi was right; some privacy would be welcome.

Levi rose, keeping a hold of her hand, and drawing her to her feet.

"Where y'all going?" Dawg asked.

"Nowhere," Levi said, and this made Dawg laugh.

Levi led Finley through the groups of people, weaving around blankets, running toddlers, and laughing teenagers. Some people waved at Levi, and others stared. He'd changed out of the baseball uniform, but everyone still recognized him. He didn't seem to let all the attention and compliments go to his psyche though, and he'd been polite to everyone who spoke to him throughout the evening. At the Little League photo op, he'd signed dozens of balls, and at the Glass Onion, he and the Six Pack were friendly to anyone who approached their table.

Finley liked the small-town feel of Belltown. And Rhett had also been fun to get to know. He was the lighter-hearted of the two brothers, and it was entertaining to see the younger brother giving the older brother a hard time. While she watched the parade with Rhett and Erin, Rhett told her she was the first woman whom Levi had introduced him to.

Finley had tried not to read too deeply into that fact. But she couldn't help but feel flattered.

"Am I getting the tour?" Finley asked Levi as they left the crowded baseball field behind.

"I thought we could watch the fireworks from the bleachers at the tennis courts."

"Then a tour?"

Levi looked down at her, his eyes dark in the moonlight. "If you want."

She nudged him. "I want."

One side of his mouth lifted. "Okay."

She grinned, and he chuckled. It took only a couple of minutes to walk to the tennis courts, and Levi kept hold of her hand the entire way. Finley liked that.

They sat in the middle of the bleachers, and Finley leaned against the row behind her, turning her gaze toward the sky. Explosions of red and white sparkled against the black night. Levi settled next to her, and she could feel the warmth from his skin even though he wasn't technically touching her.

The contrast between the coolness of the bleachers and the close proximity of Levi made goose bumps race across her arms.

"Cold?" Levi asked.

"No." She cut a glance at him. "Besides, if I were cold, what would you do?"

"There's several things I could do," he said in that low voice of his.

The goose bumps multiplied. "You don't have a jacket."

"I could give you my shirt."

Finley's face warmed, and she tried to focus on the glittery gold firework that had opened above them. "Um, I don't think I'm ready for that."

Levi lifted his hand and played with a lock of her hair. "Ready for what?"

"Ready to see Levi Cox without a shirt."

He shifted closer, and his fingers threaded through her hair. "Then I could wrap you in my arms. You know, warm you up the old-fashioned way."

She held back a smile. "That would probably work."

He moved her hair, exposing her neck. He was really close now, his thigh and hip touching hers. More fireworks exploded above, but it might as well be her pulse drumming.

Levi pressed his mouth just below her ear.

Fireworks went off in her belly.

"You smell good," he said.

After a day of heat and humidity, there was no way he could make that claim. "You're such a liar," she said.

He chuckled. "You smell like cotton candy."

Well, that made sense, she supposed. Since she did get some in her hair.

He pressed his mouth against her jaw. The scruff of his whiskers was like a prickly caress, only adding to the goose bumps racing along her skin.

"You're not watching the fireworks," she whispered, unable to stop herself from leaning into him.

He draped his arm across her shoulders. "I've seen plenty of fireworks. I'm more interested in you."

When he said things like that, she could swear her toes curled. Did he have any idea what he was doing to her? Finley exhaled and turned her head.

Levi's gaze locked with hers, and Finley gave into the temptation that had been plaguing her all day. She ran her fingers along the line of his jaw, then behind his neck. Levi watched her, not moving.

"What's happening here?" she asked.

The edge of his mouth lifted. "I think it's pretty obvious."

"I mean, beyond the obvious."

She hadn't really expected a serious answer, so she was surprised when Levi said, "I don't know exactly. This is new territory for me."

"Yeah, I kind of got that with all the teasing from your friends," she said. "And your brother said I'm the first woman you've introduced to him."

"That's true," Levi said, moving his hand down her back.

Everywhere he touched, she burned.

"So to answer your question," he murmured, "I like you, Ms. Gray. Beyond that, I can't make any predictions."

She couldn't stop the smile that bloomed. "I like you too, Mr. Florida. And I can't make any predictions either."

If anything, his gaze only intensified. "Maybe that's good enough for now."

"Maybe." She looped her other arm around his neck. Then she closed the rest of the distance and pressed her mouth against his lips in a barely-there kiss.

At that moment, a crescendo of fireworks exploded overhead. Finley drew away from Levi and looked at the sky. Whites, blues, golds, and red collided into a grand finale. From the baseball field, a rendition of the Belltown University song had started.

"Come back here," Levi said, tilting her chin toward him. This time, he kissed her.

Her entire body buzzed as he kissed her slowly, taking his time, as if there were no risk of someone passing by at any moment.

Finley rested her hands on his shoulders and kissed him back, exploring him as much as he was exploring her. His scent was warm, and she sighed into him. He drew her closer, deepening his kisses, then in one movement, his hands gripped her hips and he pulled her onto his lap.

Being this close to Levi was like an ambrosia, one she wanted more of. She pressed against him. Everything about him was delicious, and she couldn't help the moan that escaped her lips. Levi's arms completely encompassed her, and it was like he'd created an alternate world where only the two of them existed.

Voices rose and fell some distance away, and Finley clued into the fact that the crowd from the fireworks was dispersing, and their privacy would be compromised.

She drew away from Levi, and he protested, keeping her locked in his embrace.

"People are coming," she whispered.

He slowly eased his hold, and she slid off his lap.

"Come on," she said, extending her hand. "You promised me a tour."

He gazed up at her, his eyes seemingly out of focus. "I did?"

She grabbed his hand, and he rose to his feet. But instead of heading down the bleachers, he pulled her against him. She wrapped her arms about his waist and leaned into him. Closing her eyes, she listened to the steady beat of his heart. Levi's hands moved slowly up and down her back as if the last thing he wanted to do was release her.

Voices grew louder, and by the squeals and laughs, Finley guessed it was a group of teenagers.

Levi exhaled and drew away. "Okay, you're right." He linked their fingers and led her down the bleachers. "Although I'm not opposed to heading back to the hotel."

"When in Belltown..."

He shook his head, but he was smiling.

They walked slowly across the campus, and Levi pointed out the buildings where he'd had classes. When they reached the athletic department, Levi stopped. "This is where I spent most of my time," he said. "The first place I met the other guys in the Six Pack."

Only the outside lights of the building were on, so Finley couldn't see inside. "What did your brother do when you started college?"

Levi didn't answer for a moment, then he said, "He was the easy brother, you see, so he didn't have to move around as much as when I was paired with him. I worked as a school groundskeeper to get enough money together to buy him a cell phone so that we could keep in touch."

"You were a groundskeeper?"

Levi turned to face her, their hands still linked. "Yeah. Best and worst job ever."

Finley raised her brows, waiting for him to continue.

"Best, because it was outside, and I could do it solo," he said, stepping closer. "Worst, because my shift was five to eight in the morning."

Finley wrinkled her nose. "That's early. Bet that cut back on your college partying at night, right?"

"What makes you think that I was a partier?" he asked, running his thumb over her hand.

"Well, you're a beautiful man, and I'm sure the Belltown girls were knocking down your door."

"Not exactly," he said. "I was sort of moody back then. Pissed off at the world, you might say."

"No girlfriends, then?" she pressed. Knowing about Levi's past would help her figure him out. Besides, she was curious about his previous relationships. Had there been anything substantial, or were they hookups?

When Levi hesitated, Finley didn't know if she should be glad or not. Obviously, there was a story.

"I've only had one girlfriend," he said. "My junior year here. We dated a few months, and well . . ." He looked away.

Was he still hurting over the breakup?

He returned his gaze, but Finley couldn't read the expression in his eyes.

"When I told her about my past—you know, my record—she bailed."

Finley blinked. "Just like that?"

"Yep," he said. "We said goodbye that night, like usual, and after that she never answered any of my calls or texts. I waited for her outside one of her classes a couple of days later, but she ignored me when she came out."

"That's harsh," Finley said. "But I'm glad too."

Levi's brows jutted up. "What?"

"I'm glad she dumped you," Finley said, releasing his hand. She traced her fingers up his arm and over his shoulder. Then she stepped close as her hand wrapped around his neck. "Because then I wouldn't be here with you, right now."

Levi slipped his hands around her waist and pulled her flush against his body. "You make a good point." He leaned down, and Finley closed her eyes, waiting for the kiss to come.

"Steal! That you?" A voice called out of the darkness.

Levi lifted his head, and Finley moved out of his embrace.

Seconds later, two guys walked under the nearby streetlamp. Rabbit's white-blond hair was unmistakable, along with Axel Diaz's darker hair.

"What are you doing out here?" Rabbit asked, a laugh in his voice.

"Giving Finley the tour," Levi said, his voice barely civil.

"Great, we'll join you," Rabbit said.

Axel chuckled.

"Did you tell her about the time you split your pants when you stole home during the playoffs?" Rabbit asked.

"Uh, no," Levi said.

Rabbit smirked. "What about when you got so sick that you—"

Levi shoved Rabbit's shoulder, and he only laughed.

"Okay, okay," Axel cut in. "Finley would probably like to hear the *good* stories about Levi."

Rabbit grinned. "I don't think I know any."

"I think I heard Sinclairs is giving out free donuts tonight," Levi said.

"Really?" Rabbit said, slowing his step. "All night?"

"Until they run out, so you'd better hurry," Levi deadpanned.

That was all it took, and Rabbit and Axel took off, saying a quick goodbye.

Finley turned toward Levi. "What are they going to do to you when they find out the donuts aren't free?"

Levi grinned. "Not my problem."

"They're going to be pissed," Finley said.

"They'll get over it." He grasped her hand. "I have a couple more things to show you."

CHAPTER 19

LEVI SAT IN the Minnesota Ice dugout Saturday night after the game, ignoring the team congratulating each other on another win, while he pretty much admitted to himself that he'd fallen for Finley. If yesterday in Belltown was any indication of how he continually tried to get rid of his best friends in order to have Finley all to himself... And this morning.

He'd found her in the hotel workout room at six running on a treadmill. She said she had to make up for not working out the night before since she had another fight in a week. He'd convinced her to go outside with him, and they ran some of the Belltown hills. Then he'd kissed her beneath a tree at the top of a neighborhood, despite her protests that she was too sweaty.

Finally, he'd convinced her to try the donuts at Sinclairs. Watching her eat a warm glazed donut was better than eating one himself.

"Good game, Steal," Scrubs said, slapping Levi on the shoulder. "Are you camping out in the dugout tonight? Or are you going to sign some baseballs?"

"Coming," Levi said, looking up. He hadn't realized the

dugout had cleared out. His mind was not on task. At least he'd been able to focus throughout the game, although he wished Finley could have come tonight. He couldn't expect her to take both weekend nights off work for him.

Levi rose from the dugout bench. They'd barely pulled off a win tonight, beating the Wisconsin Bears by one point—a point that he'd scored by stealing home in the bottom of the eighth. He guzzled the last of his water, then stepped out of the dugout. Finley's dad, Charlie, had come and was talking to Big T.

Levi walked over and shook Charlie's hand.

"You coming to play darts?" Charlie asked.

Hanging out in a pub without Finley was the last thing he wanted to do. "Uh, I'm going to take Finley home from work. If she'll let me."

Charlie chuckled. "Good luck with that." He turned to Big T. "I'll meet you over there. I've got to stop at the gas station first."

"Sure thing, Gray," Big T said. "Bring your A game."

As Charlie headed across the infield, several other Ice players talked to him.

Levi was pleased with how Charlie had become so comfortable around the Ice players. His earlier misgivings had seemed to completely disappear.

As soon as Levi could, he escaped the crowd and headed to the team locker room. After showering, he picked up a turkey sandwich from the spread the coaches had ordered in after the game.

Then Levi headed to the parking lot and climbed into his Bronco. He still had a while before Finley would be off work, and he wasn't in the mood to sit in the pub and wait for her. He wished he could do something for her, because she'd had a long day. Well, both of their days had been long. Still.

He checked the time, although it was never too late to call Grizz.

"Hey," Grizz said when he answered his phone. "Congrats on the win."

"Thanks," Levi said. "How did the Knights fare?"

"Win." The smile in his voice was evident.

"Nice," Levi said. "I haven't checked the Six Pack texts yet."

"Sounds like you didn't call me to congratulate me on my amazing catches then," Grizz continued. "What's up, Steal?"

Levi exhaled. "Do you know anything about flowers?"

Grizz choked on a laugh. "Let me guess. You're standing at an all-night grocery store and staring at bouquets of wilted roses."

"Not quite." Levi cleared his throat. "I mean, I'm heading to the grocery store right now."

Grizz's laugh escaped. "Okay, here's the best advice I ever got. If *you* like the flowers, then Finley will like them."

"Huh." Levi thought about that. "Who told you that?"

"Mamma Sal," Grizz said. "Worked too."

Levi was surprised at this. "Do I know this story?"

"We're talking about *you* here, not me," Grizz said.

"Is Rachel part of the story we aren't talking about?" Levi asked, referring to Sawyer Bennett's sister.

Grizz chuckled. "Smooth, Cox. Why don't you turn that smoothness toward your own lady?"

Levi might have pursued the conversation, but he'd arrived at the grocery store. "Okay. I'm going in. Any more advice?"

"Don't be cheap."

Levi didn't know if he should be offended. "Did Mamma Sal tell you that too?"

"Nope," Grizz said with a chuckle. "That's directly from me to you."

So that was how Levi found himself standing before a giant, glass-doored refrigerator full of vases of flowers. He immediately dismissed the single-flower vases. Grizz would consider those cheap. Other arrangements had teddy bears or cheerful plastic messages like "Congratulations." None of those either.

His gaze locked on the roses. Orange. Pink. White. Red. The orange roses were pretty cool, and Levi stepped closer to eye the price. Thirty-nine bucks. Was that good? Was it cheap? The red roses were forty-five. Did red roses cost more to grow? And weren't red roses more of a symbol of . . . love?

Levi rubbed the back of his neck. He was pretty sure every person in the store was watching him. Although when he turned around, he didn't see one person staring.

Red. *Huh.* They definitely stood out the most in the group. The red color also reminded him of what Finley wore to the fight he'd watched. Did that mean she liked the color? Maybe the white roses would be the safer color, although white looked boring next to the red. And what Levi was doing was anything but safe.

Then he saw the discounted Fourth-of-July bouquet. The blooms had already peaked but were still vibrant. How long were flowers supposed to last anyway? A week? A few days?

"Can I help you, sir?" someone said behind him.

Reluctantly, he turned around.

A young woman with a messy blond bun stood there, her grocery store shirt smeared with something white. She must work in the nearby bakery.

"No, thanks, just looking." He walked away from the flower case and found himself staring at a rack of fishing and hunting magazines. When the employee moved on to other things, Levi went back to the flowers. It was time to make a decision and get out of there. Before he drew more notice.

Thirty minutes later, he was sitting in his Bronco in the parking lot of Finley's pub. He had a couple of hours to wait, and he supposed that he could have gone to his apartment or joined the guys and Charlie for a game of darts. But here he was, wishing Finley would walk out of the pub doors right now. Was this stalking? Likely. He decided to text Finley closer to closing time so that she didn't think he was a total stalker.

In the meantime, he settled in the front seat and closed his eyes for a short time.

A knock startled Levi awake.

It took him a second to realize he'd fallen asleep sitting in his Bronco. He turned his head to see Finley standing outside the truck, smiling at him.

Levi exhaled and popped open his door. "What time is it?" His voice came out raspy.

Finley rested her hand on the edge of the door. "One fifteen. How long have you been here?"

He rubbed at his face. "A while."

"I was going to let you sleep," she said, "since I wasn't sure if you'd come to meet me or if you were wanting to sleep in a parking lot."

Her voice was teasing, and Levi still wasn't fully awake. "I meant to text you."

She gave a soft laugh. "You know I can walk home just fine."

Levi climbed out of the truck, and Finley stepped back to give him room to stand. But he didn't want room. He grasped her hand and drew her close. "How was work tonight?"

She looked up at him and shrugged. "It's over. And your game?"

"We won."

He liked the softening he saw in her eyes. And the dimples that appeared with her smile.

"Nice," she said. "You guys are on a streak."

"Something like that." He drew her hand to his chest and clasped it there.

"You really didn't have to come, Levi." She rested her other hand on his stomach. "You need to sleep at some point."

"Sleep can wait," he said, leaning down. "I wanted to thank you for coming to Belltown."

Her lips curved right before he kissed her. For once, it was nice to not have the Six Pack around. But Finley drew away too soon.

"I don't smell too great," she said.

"Don't you think I should be the judge of that?" Levi asked, pulling her closer and burying his face in her neck. He inhaled. "French fries. Yum."

Finley laughed and tried to slug him, but Levi caught her hand and pinned it to her side while he kissed her again.

She finally relaxed and melted against him, kissing him back.

"That's better," he said, sliding both his arms about her waist.

She lifted up on her toes and wrapped her arms about his neck. He felt her smile as she kissed him, and his heart went into a full soar.

"Today's the big day," she whispered against his mouth.

He drew away to look at her. "For what?"

"For your couch," she said. "I'm hitting the garage sales at eight."

"I'm coming with you."

"You should sleep," she said. "I don't want you slacking on your game."

"I don't slack, ever."

She raised her brows.

"I'm coming with you," he repeated.

"Okay, Mr. Florida," she said, amusement in her tone. "You'd better get me home soon so that I can get some sleep."

He walked her around the Bronco, holding her hand. "What time should I pick you up?"

"Seven thirty," she said. "We have to get my dad's truck because I don't think your Bronco's going to hold a couch."

Levi opened the passenger door.

Finley moved past him, then stopped. "You got red roses?"

Levi looked at the passenger seat, where he'd buckled in the vase of flowers a couple of hours ago. "They're a thank you for coming to Belltown with me and putting up with the Six Pack."

Finley didn't move for a minute. She didn't say anything either, which made him nervous.

Should he have gone with the white? Or maybe the orange?

After another moment of absolute silence from Finley, Levi finally said, "Um, do you hate flowers, or something?"

She shook her head, then she turned toward him. She wrapped her arms around his waist and buried her face against his chest.

Levi didn't know what to say, because he was pretty sure she was crying. He pulled her close. "Are you okay?" he asked.

She shook her head, and his heart sank. Something was wrong, and he had no clue what it was.

"Did I screw up?" he whispered. "I could take them back or throw them in the Dumpster over there."

She laughed, or maybe it was a sob. But she didn't move from clinging to him, so he rubbed her back slowly.

"I'm sorry," he said finally, because in truth, he was at a complete loss. Didn't women like flowers? Wasn't it a sign of appreciation?

"Don't be sorry," Finley said, her voice soft. She drew away and wiped her eyes. "I don't know what's wrong with me. I love the flowers. I do, really. You're sweet, Levi, and kind of overwhelming."

He stared at her. How was he supposed to take that? "I don't mean to be overwhelming. Wait. Is that a good thing or bad thing?"

Her lips edged into a smile. "It's just what it is. I don't expect flowers, or you giving me a ride home after work in the middle of the night." She exhaled. "You introduced me to all your friends, and your brother, and . . ."

Levi waited.

"You're making it really hard to stay angry."

He lifted his brows. "Angry about what?"

"A lot of things," she said in a quiet voice. "Everything."

Strangely, he understood. Perfectly. "You're making it hard for me to stay angry too. Buying flowers was a new experience for me, and I think I'd like to do it again, if you let me. And if it doesn't make you cry."

Finley gave him a tentative smile. "I think I'd still cry."

He lowered his head and rested his forehead against hers. She closed her eyes, and neither of them moved for a moment.

"Thank you for the roses, Levi," she whispered. "I love them."

"You're welcome."

Grizz had been right. Levi had picked his favorite, and Finley had liked them too.

Chapter 20

"Your couch is almost done," Finley told Levi over the phone.

"You work fast," he said, his low voice reaching through the phone like a caress.

Finley was sitting on said couch, in the dark, at one thirty in the morning. Talking to Levi was the next best thing to seeing him. With Levi traveling for games, Finley had hyper focused on working on his couch and added in extra training sessions.

She'd be fighting Shirley Temple in about twenty-two hours. And Levi was coming to watch. If his plane was on time. He was playing an afternoon game in North Dakota and said he'd fly back to Minneapolis right after.

"Work was good?" he asked.

"Work was work," she said. "Not as exciting as your triple home run."

"Got lucky, that's all," Levi said.

"Well, I'm going to need some of that luck."

"You'll be fine," he said. "I hardly get to see you, you train so much."

"Ha. Ha. You're the one who keeps flying around the country."

She heard the smile in Levi's voice when he said, "You can always travel with me."

Finley scoffed, although she was flattered. "And be a groupie? No thanks."

"Not a groupie. My girlfriend." His tone was serious.

Her breath stalled. "What are you saying, Mr. Florida?"

"Well . . . I did get you flowers," he said in his low, sexy voice. "And you are fixing up a couch for me. Also, your dad likes me, or maybe it's Big T and Scrubs."

Finley laughed. "He likes you, too."

"Then it sounds like a no-brainer," he said. "Unless you changed your mind about liking me."

She couldn't help but grin. "I haven't changed my mind."

"Me either."

Her heart was thumping so hard, she wouldn't be surprised if Levi could hear it through her cell phone.

"So . . ." It was a question.

"Okay, Mr. Florida," she said. "I guess we're official. Are you going to post it to social media?"

He laughed. "There's no one on social media that I care to know my business."

Warmth buzzed through Finley, and if she'd been standing, she would have jelly legs. Were they really doing this?

"But I'd do it for you," Levi continued.

Finley wondered if she'd ever stop smiling long enough to get some sleep tonight. "No, *please no*."

Levi chuckled, then said in a quiet tone, "I can't wait to see you."

Finley closed her eyes, her heart feeling like it might run right out of her body. "Well, go to sleep because then it will happen a lot sooner."

When she finally hung up with Levi, she knew she'd officially lost her heart to him. It had crept up on her bit by bit. She'd never imagined that she'd be able to allow someone into her heart other than her father.

For her entire life, she'd kept everyone outside of her dad and grandparents at an arm's length. No girlfriends. No serious boyfriends. No attachments. And she'd worked out her frustrations and deep pain through exercising. Her intense workouts kept her going one more day, one more week, and got rid of the anger she never quite knew what to do with when it collected.

Anger at her mom. Anger for her abandoned dad. Anger at an unfair world and cruel people.

But Levi had slowly, almost imperceptibly, been changing that.

She'd never felt so . . . whole. She'd never felt this source of constant hope. She'd never been friends with anyone at this deeper level, as she was with Levi.

Finley didn't move from the couch she was finishing for Levi. She'd be done Sunday and would deliver it then. Right now, having it in her place was like keeping Levi close to her.

When Finley next opened her eyes, the sun was blazing through the window she'd forgotten to lower the blinds on. She sat up with a start. Her phone read nine thirty, which didn't give her time to do yoga before reporting to her shift.

She scrolled through some missed texts.

Her dad said he was coming to her match tonight. Finley texted him a thumbs up.

At 7:00 a.m., Levi had texted, *Good morning, girlfriend.*

Their conversation from the night before tumbled in—every word—and it made Finley feel breathless even though she had yet to leave the couch. It appeared Levi hadn't forgotten either, or changed his mind. Anticipation buzzed through Finley as she calculated the number of hours until her match—the number of hours it would be before she saw Levi again.

As she suspected, the next hours dragged by. The pub was busy, like a usual Saturday, but Finley only felt more and more amped up. Both her dad and Levi were coming to her match, and she wanted to win this one over Shirley Temple. The take-home was four hundred, and Finley would be more than happy with that.

She checked the brass clock above the bar dozens of times, waiting for the magic time of eleven thirty, when Mark said she could leave and get ready for the match. Only a few minutes to go now.

"Ma'am?" a guy at one of the tables in her section called out to her. He had one of those bushy goatees that made him look like he was trying too hard.

Finley held up her finger to indicate she'd be with him in a second as she closed out another order.

The guy tipped back his chair and said in a louder voice, "Can a man get some service around here? I've been waiting ten minutes for a drink."

The back of Finley's neck prickled. It hadn't been close to ten minutes since she'd taken the guy his second beer.

Patrons at the nearby tables had taken notice of the blond man with his overgrown goatee. Finley wasn't about to let him cause a scene. She turned from the register and caught Mark's gaze. He raised his brows, and she nodded. She'd take care of it.

On the way to Goatee Guy's table, she stopped by the bar and asked the bartender for another bottle. She crossed the room, then set the bottle in front of Goatee Guy, along with his tab.

"Final drink, sir," she said. "Bar's closed."

His bloodshot eyes narrowed. "Doesn't look closed to me, ma'am."

Finley tapped the bill she'd set on the table. "Cash or card?"

Goatee Guy's eyes roamed over her. "I'll let you know when I'm ready to leave." He picked up the beer and drank half of it down. "You gonna watch me now? Where was all this attention ten minutes ago? How about you get me another one instead of standing around—"

"Like she said, bar's closed."

Finley snapped her gaze up to see Levi.

He wasn't looking at her, but solely focused on Goatee Guy. And now Finley knew what a baseman must see when Levi was getting ready to steal a base.

"You work here?" Goatee Guy said. "Can you be my waiter? Hopefully you're faster on your feet than this chick—"

He didn't finish, because Levi grasped the guy's collar and dragged him to his feet.

The guy's eyes popped open, then his face reddened. On instinct, Finley knew what the guy was going to do before he moved his arm. He threw a right hook, aiming for Levi. It all happened so fast that Finley wasn't sure how she'd gotten in between the two men. Finley blocked Goatee Guy's fist with her left hand, then socked him in the gut with her right.

Goatee Guy doubled over, gasping for air. "You b—"

"You need to leave right now." Mark had appeared, and he grabbed the guy's arm. "One more word, and I'm calling the cops."

The guy wheezed as Mark propelled him toward the door, Levi following.

Finley stood in one place, her adrenaline spiking, as Mark and Levi escorted the jerk outside. It took her a second before she realized people in the pub were clapping. For her. She exhaled, then turned and nodded to a few of them as she headed to the kitchen. Her shift was over.

"Did that just happen?" Jensen said, intercepting her before she pushed through the kitchen door.

"I'm not sure what happened," Finley said. "He was going to hit Levi."

Jensen grinned. "So you punched him first, to protect *Levi Cox*?"

Finley released a shaky breath. "I guess."

Jensen chuckled. "I think Cox could have taken care of himself."

Of course he could have. She couldn't talk about this right now. Her head was spinning. "I'm off. Gotta get ready for the fight."

"I think you're warmed up," Jensen said.

Finley grimaced and pushed through the kitchen doors. She wanted to go outside the pub, to see what Levi and Mark were doing. Had Goatee Guy left?

She tugged off her apron, and when she left the kitchen, Mark had come back in. He did a quick scan of her. "Are you okay?" he asked.

"Yeah, where's Levi?"

"Don't worry about that," Mark said. "You should have let me handle that guy. I don't want brawls at the pub."

Finley's face heated. "It wasn't a brawl. What did you tell Levi?"

"I told him to leave and cool off," Mark said. "I'm sure he doesn't want charges, and neither do you."

"It was self-defense," Finley said, lifting her chin.

"Levi grabbed him first." Mark fixed her with a hard look. "Next time, let *me* handle it. Things could have gotten much worse."

She nodded, although she wasn't convinced another outcome would have been possible. Especially with the look she'd seen in Levi's eyes. She headed to the back of the pub and went down the steps that led to the basement. A few people had already gathered, but she ignored them as she went into the back room where she'd stashed her boxing stuff.

She felt numb as she changed her clothes. Worst-case scenarios flashed through her mind. What if she hadn't blocked the guy's punch? Or Mark hadn't shown up when he did? Levi would have retaliated, and things would have gotten uglier.

Finley went into her first yoga position and closed her eyes. This was not how tonight was supposed to go. And where was Levi now?

She straightened and grabbed her phone, then called Levi. No answer.

Finley tossed the phone onto the ratty chair in the corner.

She'd have to figure things out later. After the fight.

The noise volume increased in the main room, and Finley could only guess that Shirley Temple had arrived. Music started up, thumping its way through the walls.

Finley focused on her breathing, finding her center as she stretched. Levi or not, her dad would be at the fight. And Finley was planning on using her adrenaline from the pub incident to knock out Shirley Temple as soon as possible.

When Mark's voice boomed into the microphone, Finley was as ready as she was going to get. She pulled on her robe, then strapped on her gloves.

Leaving the room, she stopped in the corridor.

Shirley Temple was standing next to the door, wearing a yellow, satin robe, her thick, curly hair braided tightly against her head. Shirley nodded when she saw Finley, but the women didn't exchange words.

Mark announced "Fin," so Finley passed Shirley and stepped out into the room. As Mark went through her thin resume of success, Finley scanned the area. There was her dad . . . next to Levi.

Finley couldn't describe the relief she felt at seeing Levi. Not that she thought he was going to aggravate the earlier situation more and end up arrested. Okay, so she had definitely worried that he'd do something to get arrested.

But he was here. By her dad.

Levi's arms were folded and his jaw set. His gaze bored into hers, and she had to look away because her mind should be focused on the upcoming match. Not whether Levi was pissed at her.

Finley entered the boxing ring and lifted her hand in acknowledgment for those who clapped for her.

Next, Mark introduced Shirley Temple. Her reception was less than Star's had been a couple of weeks ago, so it appeared that Finley had an equal number of fans tonight.

Shirley was strong, but Finley knew how to wear her out. It would be a matter of who could stay on their feet the longest.

Finley kept moving to keep her body warmed up. She rotated her neck and shoulders, then focused on Shirley Temple. The woman was about an inch taller than Finley, but Shirley always crouched as she boxed, which Finley planned to take advantage of.

Mark announced the beginning of the match, and both boxers moved to the middle and faced each other. The ref joined the women and reviewed the rules, mostly for the crowd. When the ref stepped away, Mark rang the bell, and the fight had officially started.

Shirley swung immediately, and Finley barely dodged the blow. She recovered and delivered a blow of her own, striking Shirley in the shoulder before she could draw back.

First contact had been made, which meant they wouldn't be wasting time circling each other. Shirley swung again, and this time Finley blocked the blow, and with her other hand, she delivered an upper cut to Shirley's jaw.

Shirley's head snapped back, and she staggered, but then righted herself. And charged.

Finley spun to the side, then drove her glove into the back of Shirley's shoulder. Shirley retaliated and punched Finley in the stomach.

The air whooshed out of her. As she doubled over to gulp in air, Shirley drove her glove into the side of Finley's face. She almost went down, but it was by sheer determination, or luck, that Finley stayed on her feet. Miraculously, the bell rang, ending the first round.

Finley walked to her corner, feeling like she was swaying more than walking a straight line.

To her surprise, her dad was there. With water and an ice pack.

She sat and drank the water while her dad pressed the pack against the side of her face.

"It's swelling," he said. "Can you still see?"

Finley blinked against the sweat. "I can see."

"Time's up," her dad said, lowering the ice pack and patting her shoulder. "Now get out there and take Temple down."

Finley nodded and rose to her feet. The dizziness had passed, but she was sure more would come. Shirley Temple's eyes had darkened, and vertical lines had appeared between her brows.

Finley joined Shirley Temple in the center, and this time Finley got in the first swing. Her glove connected with Shirley's jaw. Immediately, Finley stepped to the side, getting out of Shirley's retaliation. But Shirley lunged and locked herself around Finley, pounding into her ribcage. Pain jacked through Finley's torso, but she wrestled away, then slammed her glove above Shirley's ear. At first, Finley expected Shirley to spin away and recover. But the woman's knees buckled, and she collapsed.

Finley stared as Mark counted down with the help of the crowd.

"Fin takes the match!" Mark hollered into the microphone.

Everyone was cheering, "Fin! Fin! Fin!"

Finley's head buzzed with disbelief. She should be happy. Elated. But only a dull ache had taken over her mind. Things hurt and throbbed on her body, and she knew the pain hadn't fully surfaced yet.

Her dad's face came into view as he moved to the front of the crowd. Finley didn't have the energy to look for Levi. She'd only boxed two rounds, but suddenly she was very tired.

Mark continued giving her accolades in the microphone, recapping the two rounds, and Shirley Temple was being checked over by her trainer.

Not really caring what happened next, Finley left the ring and went into the back room. She entered the small bathroom and splashed water on her face and arms. Then she grabbed a couple of paper towels and pressed them against her face, keeping her eyes closed.

She focused on her breathing, focused on calming her heart rate. She didn't want to return to the crowd and hear their praises and accept the bounty. She was more than ready to call it a night.

CHAPTER 21

LEVI PUSHED THROUGH the crowd celebrating Finley's win. She'd left the ring and disappeared through the back door. Was she going to change, then return and celebrate? Levi didn't know, and it looked like her dad was busy chatting with other people.

So Levi made his way around the crowd and opened the door that Finley had disappeared through. No one questioned him or stopped him, not that anyone would be able to.

He found her sitting on a low bench, packing her gloves into a duffle bag. She'd pulled on yoga pants and a cropped T-shirt over her boxing outfit. She looked up, and he winced at the sight of the bruising that had darkened across her cheek and around her eye.

"You okay?" Finley asked.

"*Me?*" Levi stopped in front of her. "You just won a boxing match, and you're asking if *I'm* okay?"

She looked down at the bag and zipped it up. "When you went outside, I was afraid that you . . ."

She didn't need to finish.

A rock had settled into Levi's stomach. "You thought I'd

assault the guy? Add to my record?" He hadn't meant his voice to sound bitter, but that was how it came out.

Finley didn't respond. She rose to her feet, now closer to him, and shouldered her bag. An unmistakable flash of pain crossed her face.

Levi reached for the bag and almost expected her to move away from him, but she let him take it.

"Are you going back out there?" he asked.

"No." Her brown eyes focused on him, and in them, he saw the questions she wasn't asking.

And this small basement room wasn't the place to talk.

"Want a ride home?" he asked in a quieter voice.

She blinked, breaking her intense focus on him. Then she nodded.

The rock in Levi's stomach lightened. Maybe things were okay. Maybe she didn't think he was such a loose screw. But, in truth, despite his rollercoaster life, he'd never felt angrier than he had when he'd overheard what that idiot in the pub had said to Finley tonight. That's why Levi had to leave for a while. Not to punch the guy's lights out—which would have been nice—but to put some distance between himself and his intense emotions.

It was only after he saw Finley's dad arrive at the pub that Levi decided to attend the match. Then it was all he could do to not intervene after that first round and tell her to back out of the match. He hadn't been in any mood to watch her get beat up—even if it was a women's boxing match.

But through his turbulent emotions, he knew there was no way he could ask that of Finley. He wasn't being logical or reasonable. Maybe he did have a loose screw.

Finley led the way along the corridor to the back door that led to another exit, taking them to the parking lot. Levi followed. Finley didn't speak, and it was better if he didn't right now either.

When they reached his Bronco, Levi opened the passenger door for her, and she let him help her in. As he drove, she pulled out her phone and texted someone. He assumed it was her dad, or Mark, or both.

Leaving the site of the pub was already helping Levi feel more calm. He parked at the curb in front of her building, then opened his door. She hadn't invited him up, but she hadn't uninvited him either. When they reached her apartment, Finley unlocked the door and flipped on the lights as she went inside. Levi stopped in the doorway.

A couch sat halfway between the kitchen and living room, probably because that was the only place it would fit among all the other furniture pieces.

"It's not finished yet," Finley said, walking around it and heading toward the kitchen.

The fabric was some sort of dark-gray suede, and the wood frame had been painted or stained a deep brown, almost black. The cushions had all been re-covered, and the sides and bottom tacked on. But the suede fabric draped over the back hadn't been fastened yet.

Levi walked over to inspect it. "This is amazing."

Finley didn't answer, but she opened the freezer and pulled out a bag of ice.

"I can get that," he said. "You should sit down."

She turned to face him, the ice bag still in hand. "Do you like the color?"

He crossed to her and took the ice bag. "Since it's my favorite color, I love it."

The edge of her mouth lifted, and Levi considered it progress.

"Come on, you should be sitting down." He grasped her

hand, and she let him draw her to the couch that belonged permanently in her apartment.

She sat down, then he went to prepare an ice bag and found a dishcloth to use between her skin and the ice. When he returned she was leaning her head against the couch, her eyes closed.

He sat a cushion away from her and said, "Lie down."

She opened an eye, then scooted so that she put her head on his leg. He set the cloth over half of her face, then carefully put on the ice bag.

"You don't have to play nurse," she said.

"You don't always get to order me around."

Her smile was faint, but it was there.

Levi smoothed the hair from her forehead. "Does anything else hurt?"

"My back aches some, but the thing that hurts most is my wrist, where I blocked Goatee Guy's punch to your throat."

"Goatee Guy?"

"I don't know his name."

"Next time, don't stand between me and a guy who wants to throw a punch," he said. "If he'd hit you, he'd be in the hospital, and I'd be in jail right now."

Finley lifted her hand and removed the ice bag. She blinked up at him. "He wasn't worth it."

"Which is exactly why I can't figure out why you thought you could take him on," Levi said.

"I . . ." She paused. "I guess I thought if he hit you, and you hit him back, then the cops would come . . . Like that time you were arrested in another pub."

Levi exhaled. "This is exactly why I normally stay away from pubs."

"I know." She pushed herself into a sitting position, unable to hide her wince.

"Do you want some aspirin?" he asked.

"I already took some," she said.

He wanted to do something for her, anything. "Do you want a bath?"

One of her brows lifted, the one not surrounded by bruising. "You're going to draw me a bath?"

He couldn't tell if she wanted to laugh at his offer—or maybe she was surprised. "If you want me to, I will."

She moved closer and placed a hand on his chest. His heart thumped in response, and goose bumps raced across his skin at her touch.

"Don't start fights in pubs anymore," she whispered.

His lips twitched. "I'm working on that weakness."

She smiled at last, those dimples appearing, and he leaned closer, gauging for her reaction. He wanted to kiss her, but was she in too much pain?

"Am I too ugly to kiss?" she asked.

He ran his fingers along her neck, careful to avoid any place she might be hurting. "Never." Pressing a soft kiss on her mouth was about all he could allow himself to do. He didn't want to cause her any more pain.

"I think you can do better than that, Mr. Florida," she said, sliding her hand up his chest, then around his neck.

So he kissed her for real. Keeping in mind that she'd just finished a boxing match. She was warm, and she smelled of hand soap she must have used after the fight, but he didn't mind. She was Finley, the woman he was falling in love with. And he was pretty sure she'd forgiven him for the incident in the pub, because she was kissing him back too.

Levi slid his hands around her waist, over the skin that had been exposed by her cropped T-shirt. Then he moved one hand up her back, and she drew in her breath sharply.

He pulled away. "Sorry."

"I think I cracked a rib."

Levi stared at her. "You *cracked a rib* . . . and you're trying to make out with me?"

Finley laughed, then she winced again. "Don't make me laugh."

"Turn around," Levi said, and she obeyed.

He lifted the back of her shirt and pressed his fingers lightly along each of her ribs until she said, "That one!"

"I'm taking you to the doctor," Levi said.

"No, it's the middle of the night," she said. "Besides, there's nothing they'll do for a cracked rib. Just tell me to ice it and take ibuprofen."

Levi knew that, and apparently Finley did too.

He lowered her shirt. "You should still get x-rayed."

"Maybe tomorrow," she said, looking over at him.

He nodded, but he still wished she wasn't being so stubborn. "So, an ice bath?"

"Stop fussing over me." She moved close again and laid her head on his lap.

He replaced the ice bag on her face.

She linked one of her hands with his and closed her good eye.

He watched her for a moment, then he said, "Are you ever going to tell me why you fight? You didn't even stay to accept congratulations after beating Shirley Temple."

Her words came slowly. "Like I said, it burns off my energy."

Levi pulled her hand to his lips and pressed a kiss on her knuckles. "You did say you'd be my girlfriend, so I was hoping for a real answer."

She cracked an eye open. Closed it again. Then she exhaled.

He waited.

"I told you my mom left when I was a kid," she said.

"Yeah."

"My dad was enough for a long time," she continued in a quiet voice. "But then one day, he wasn't enough. I wanted a mom too. I watched the kids at school get picked up by their moms. Moms who'd come in and do reading time, or put together a class party, or bring cookies to the school fund-raisers."

She stopped talking again, but Levi waited for her to continue.

"When I was about eleven, I got in an argument with the prettiest girl in class," Finley said. "She made me so mad that I punched her. She started bawling, of course, and I got into big trouble. By my teacher and principal, at least. My dad was mad, but he was kind of impressed too. When he got me home that day, he said maybe I should be a boxer someday."

Levi raised his brows. "Your dad said that?"

"He was kidding," she said. "But it made me curious. I started watching women's boxing. And it sent a rush of adrenaline through me every time I watched. And I wanted to do the punching."

"Get all that energy out," Levi said.

She removed the ice pack again, and he set it on the cushion on the other side. "But now it's different," she said in a quiet voice.

This surprised him. "What do you mean?"

She held his gaze for a moment. "I thought winning Shirley Temple would be amazing, make me *feel* amazing. Happy too. But it didn't."

Levi traced the edge of her jaw, then rested his hand on her neck. "What are you saying?"

"I don't know what I'm saying," she said. "Maybe I'm tired. But I do know that since I've met you, the anger hasn't been the same. I don't know if it's all the way gone, but a lot of it is."

Levi leaned down and pressed a kiss on her forehead. "I don't think anyone has ever told me something so nice."

Her smile was faint, and she closed her eyes again. She didn't say anything more, and Levi was pretty sure she was falling asleep. He also didn't want to make her move again. So when her breathing evened out, he leaned his head against the couch and closed his own eyes.

CHAPTER 22

"ARE YOU SURE about this, Fin?" her dad said as they waited together on the street corner for Levi to show up. The summer day was already plenty warm at eight in the morning.

Levi and her dad were moving his couch to his apartment today, then the rest of the furniture to the swap meet, where Finley hoped to sell every last piece she'd been working on for the past month. Levi had pretty much forced her to get an X-ray, and it turned out she had two bruised ribs. Nothing cracked or broken, but Levi wouldn't let her lift anything.

So her dad had showed up with Chad and Brent to move the furniture out of her apartment, although they'd already taken off. Now, Finley looked down at the couch she'd rebuilt for Levi, although she knew that her dad was referring to more than just making furniture. More than the fact that she and Levi were exclusively dating. Levi had invited her to one of his out-of-town games against the Black Racers—Sawyer Bennett's team. They'd fly to Ohio after the swap meet.

Going with Levi to the game would be another step in the relationship department. Another level up. He told her she could sit in the family section with the wives and girlfriends of some of the players. He'd also invited her dad, but he'd opted out.

"I'm sure," she finally said. "Levi's not perfect. But neither am I."

Her dad nodded. "I know how you are around other people, especially women."

Finley rested her hands on her hips. "I'm not going to punch any of the women."

He chuckled. "Are you sure about that?"

She smirked. "I'll keep my best waitressing manners about me."

"Good," he said, then he hesitated, and Finley couldn't let that pass.

"What else are you worried about, Dad?" she pressed.

He shoved his hands into the pockets of his loose jeans. "You've never been like this before ... had a boyfriend. I worry about you getting hurt. I mean, I know Levi's smitten with you. But things happen."

"Then this road trip will be a good test for us, right?"

Her dad looked away for a moment, then back to Finley. "Right. I . . . I know I was lacking as a parent, and I hope you didn't get too jaded growing up."

Finley frowned. "What do you mean?"

"I know why you box," he said.

The statement shouldn't have bothered Finley, but it sort of did. "Yeah, well, it's better than turning to other self-medicating methods."

Her dad's gaze was sharp. "Maybe I should have taken you to a psychologist or something. Or brought you to Minnesota sooner to get away from those bullying girls."

Finley stared at her dad. His tone was remorseful. Was he really regretting so much? "We both did the best we knew how, Dad." She walked over to him and put her arms around him. "You're the best dad. And I would hate it if you were perfect. Mom left both of us, and we stuck together. You've been my rock my whole life, so don't go changing that now because I have a boyfriend."

Her dad hugged her back. "Thanks, Fin. I don't know where I'd be in life without you. Definitely not standing on this corner so early in the morning."

She laughed and squeezed him, then released him as she heard the recognizable sound of the Bronco approaching. "By the way," she told her dad, "I might be giving up boxing."

"What?" her dad said. "When did you decide that?"

"I've been thinking about it," Finley said. "Nothing's decided."

The Bronco was closer, and Finley knew she only had a few more seconds to talk to her dad alone. "Don't say anything to Levi. I want to be sure."

Her dad nodded. "Okay, honey. Whatever you think is best. I'll miss it, but I won't miss worrying about you getting hurt."

She gave her dad a grateful smile, then turned as Levi stopped his Bronco at the curb. He'd hitched a flatbed trailer to the back. When he climbed out, with a smile on that gorgeous face of his, Finley went all weak-kneed.

She rested a hand on the back of his new couch for good measure.

"Hi, Charlie," Levi said, his smile cutting from Finley to her dad.

"Cox, you're late," her dad said.

Levi chuckled. "Only you would think ten minutes early is actually late."

Her dad grinned. "True."

Levi crossed to Finley, and right there in front of her dad, he kissed her cheek. Finley's face grew warm because she was thinking of other things he could have done too. She didn't meet her dad's eyes as she stepped away from the couch. "Get to work, gentlemen."

She watched as Levi and her dad hoisted the couch into the trailer. Then Levi strapped the thing down with long bungee cords. On the drive over to his apartment, Finley sat in the back, letting her dad take the front seat so that he could drill Levi on the upcoming game against the Black Racers.

Then the questioning turned to the Six Pack, since Sawyer Bennett of the Black Racers was one of the pitchers.

"You're all still good friends?" her dad asked.

"Yeah," Levi said. "We don't see each other as much as a whole group anymore. Maybe two to three times a year, but some of our teams play each other, and we keep in touch by phone."

"They must be like your family," her dad mused.

"Next to my brother, they're the only family I've had."

Finley wondered what her dad was driving at, but she didn't want to ask him in front of Levi. Her dad was acting more introspective than usual.

Once they reached Levi's apartment, he handed her his keys, and she went ahead of the men carrying the couch to unlock the door. She held the door wide as Levi and her dad tipped the couch sideways, then wrestled it through the door.

"Oh, wow," her dad said, looking around before Levi directed him to which wall to set the couch against. "Did you just move here?"

Levi chuckled. "That's what Finley asked. I've been here four years."

"Huh." Her dad wiped at his forehead. "Do you at least have a bed?"

"I do," Levi said. "And a washer and dryer."

"Well, I agree with Finley, you definitely could use a couch."

Finley smirked and cast Levi a glance.

He simply nodded. "Well, who wants to do the honors?"

"You first," Finley and her dad said at the same time to Levi.

Levi grinned. "All right, here it goes." He moved to the couch and sat right in the middle. "So far, so good."

Finley's dad sat on one end of the couch. "It's nice."

Levi patted the cushion next to him, and Finley sat there.

"Much better," she said. "Maybe you'll have more friends now."

"I don't want more friends," Levi said. "You two keep me plenty busy."

Her dad chuckled. "Well, I'm hungry. Let's go get breakfast before we load up the rest of the stuff for the swap meet." He stood and walked toward the door, taking another look around. "You might want a coffee table and another chair in here."

"I'm on it," Finley said.

"I wouldn't expect anything less," her dad said with a wink. "Meet you in the Bronco."

"That was weird," Finley said after her dad left. "He must really be hungry."

"Or . . ." Levi said, reaching for her hand. "He's letting us celebrate my new couch."

She arched a brow. "What do you mean?"

"How're your ribs?" he asked.

"Getting better," she said before Levi pulled her close and kissed her.

This was no time to go all melty, since her dad was waiting for them, but her body wasn't listening to her brain. She moved her hands through Levi's hair and breathed in his clean scent, kissing him back.

"Thanks for the couch," he whispered. "I love it, and I love you on it."

Finley's stomach did all kinds of fluttery things, and she wouldn't have minded staying here, in Levi's arms, but their day was packed. And her dad was waiting.

"You're welcome, Mr. Florida," she said. "Be prepared for more furniture."

He gave a mock groan, and she laughed. Then she pushed against his chest. "We're on a schedule today."

"I know." He kissed her again, briefly, with only a little bit of lingering. Then he rose to his feet and held out his hand.

When he'd pulled her to her feet, she turned to survey the couch against the wall. "Much better."

"Um-hmm." He snaked his arms around her from behind.

She leaned against him, relishing in the feel of his solid, strong body behind her. "We really have to go."

He exhaled. "Okay."

They left the apartment, and Finley hated that she had to stand by while the men did all the work of loading and unloading the furniture. While she watched. And bossed them around.

The swap meet was busy by the time they were all set up, and even though Finley had told Levi he didn't need to stay for the selling part, he stayed.

Which brought a lot more attention than usual. Because he was a professional baseball player, and it seemed that a lot of swap-meet customers were baseball fans.

Every single one of Finley's furniture pieces sold in two hours, and she didn't need to discount a single item. Levi and her dad chatted with customers, and Finley answered their questions about the refinishing work.

When the last piece had been sold, a coffee table that

Finley had inlaid with broken pottery pieces in a mosaic pattern, her dad said, "Well, that's that. Anyone want a cold soda?"

"I'll take a water," Finley said.

"Me too," Levi added.

"You're making me rich, Mr. Florida," she said as her dad walked away.

"That's my plan," Levi said, turning to her with a smile. "Then you can quit the pub."

Finley gazed into his dark-green eyes. "That's your plan, huh?"

"Yeah." He stepped closer, his expression completely serious. "You don't need to cater to drunk jerks every night. I've seen your excitement over this furniture stuff. Maybe you could do that full time?"

"Did you see my place?" she said. "I couldn't have fit one more thing in there, even if I could afford to get more garage-sale pieces." She waved a hand. "And this is only once a month, four months of the year."

"Could you sell your stuff online or maybe open a storefront?"

Finley stared at him. Yeah, maybe she'd thought it would be awesome to do what she loved full-time. But what Levi was talking about would take a huge investment. Even if her dad put in money and she got a bank loan, it would be risky at best. She couldn't imagine how long it might take to see any sort of profit to replace her current income.

"If I moved in with my dad, maybe," she said. "But I don't think I could make that type of sacrifice, no matter how much I love him."

"Understood," Levi said. "But what if you had an investor?"

Her brows shot up. "I'm a nobody, Levi Cox. Without a

year-round swap meet, I'd have to come up with a proven selling strategy first. That might take a year or two, especially if I were to talk to a venture capitalist."

His gaze didn't move from her. "I meant a private investor."

She didn't respond right away, because her mind was reeling. "You mean *you*."

His smile was slow. "Yes."

She exhaled. He couldn't possibly be offering . . . yet here he was. Offering.

"I'm good with numbers," he said, slipping his hand in hers. "We could rent out a space. Maybe a storage unit or even a section in a warehouse. Something that wouldn't be too cold, so you could work through the winter. My brother's in a bunch of marketing classes he keeps telling me about. He could help us figure out an online store."

Finley felt like her chest had expanded, and her mind had flooded with dozens of scenarios and possibilities. "I don't know," she said at last. "It's a lot to think about."

"I agree," he said. "So think about it."

Her dad arrived, and Levi squeezed her hand and let go.

Finley took the water bottle from her dad and drank most of it down. Had Levi really offered to invest in a business? *Her* business? He'd barely gotten a couch in his apartment—a refurbished couch at that. How could she expect him to put thousands of dollars into *her* dream?

Chapter 23

Levi could tell Finley was nervous, although she greeted everyone he introduced her to with a smile. Her waitressing smile. He hoped that would change soon and that Finley would enjoy being around the other wives and girlfriends and family members of the Minnesota Ice team.

Levi was hesitant to leave her in the stands, but warm-ups were starting soon, and he had to get down to the field. Plus, he didn't want to hover.

"We'll keep her safe," Ashley, Kaelin's girlfriend, said, waving him off.

"Yeah, you need to get down there," Finley added, taking her seat and putting more distance between them. Her smile didn't quite reach her eyes, but there was nothing else Levi could do at this point.

He'd asked her to come, she'd agreed, and now they were in the Columbus Black Racers stadium. "See you after the game, then," Levi said, moving up the aisle.

All eyes were on him, but he didn't care. Finley was who he cared about. Not gossip from others.

As he headed toward the field, he realized it was

important to him that Finley feel comfortable around the extended Ice family. He wanted to be with her more, and that included her coming to his away games. Maybe if he could talk her into going into furniture refurbishing full-time, her schedule wouldn't be tied to the open hours of a pub. She'd be more flexible. To travel with him.

Levi might be jumping a dozen steps ahead in his mind in his relationship with Finley, but if there was one thing for certain, it was that he wanted her in his life. And more than driving her home from work at one in the morning.

"Thought you were going to watch the game instead of playing," someone called out as Levi reached the field.

Levi looked over at the Black Racers dugout to see Sawyer Bennett. The tall, lanky pitcher grinned, his blue eyes filled with confidence.

"Hey, Skeet," Levi said. "Ready to lose our bet?"

Skeeter came the rest of the way out of the dugout and straightened to his full height, an inch or so taller than Levi. "Loser rolls in the Black Racer stadium dirt? Is that the one you're talking about?"

"The very one." Levi smirked.

"I hope your girlfriend likes her man covered in red dirt, then," Skeet said, brows raised.

"The only dirt on my uniform will be from stealing your bases."

Skeet chuckled. "Hey, so all bets aside, what are you doing after the game?"

Levi rubbed the back of his neck. "The team's going out, but I'm sure Finley will be tired of everyone by then."

"And you."

Levi cracked a smile. "Especially me."

"Then come over to my place," Skeet said. "I'll throw something on the grill."

"You? Cook?"

Skeet shrugged. "I've learned a thing or two since college, and Erica might have showed me a little something too."

"*Teach?* Where is she tonight?"

"Happens to be at a teacher's training," Skeet said, his smile coy.

Levi grinned. "Still can't believe she's a teacher. She was the smartest of us all at Belltown, though, so I guess it makes sense. Plus, a dang good tutor." Erica had pretty much been the official Six Pack tutor. She'd helped Levi more than once with complicated assignments.

"Also, I've got a pool and hot tub," Skeet continued. "If, you know, you and Finley want to try it out."

"Subtle," Levi deadpanned.

"The invite's there, just sayin'," Skeet said. "Free food and the best company in Ohio."

"Sure, why not?" Levi said. "As long as Finley's okay with it."

"You're a good boyfriend," Skeet said, "putting the lady's wishes first. Don't tell me you're still getting advice from Grizz."

Levi chuckled. "He might be able to teach you a thing or two."

"That'll be the day." Skeet slapped Levi's arm. "Better get out there before your coach's face gets any redder. I don't think he likes you talking to the opposing team's pitcher."

"He won't mind when I hit a home run off you." Levi jogged to the visiting team's dugout and grabbed his mitt that he'd left there. Then he joined the warm-ups with his team.

He mostly focused on what he was doing, but a few times he glanced over at Finley. She seemed to be interacting with the other women and family members. Maybe she wasn't having a terrible time. Maybe he was worrying for nothing.

It turned out that Skeeter got to do the honors and roll in the dirt. Finley was standing next to Levi, holding his hand, when Skeet paid his dues.

"You guys are nuts," Finley said with a laugh. "I mean really nuts."

Skeeter climbed to his feet and held out his arms. "Good enough, Steal?"

"Get used to it," Levi said, snapping a picture to send to the Six Pack text strand. "We play tomorrow night too."

Skeet grimaced. "And I'm not pitching, so we shouldn't be betting on anything."

Levi shrugged. "Not my problem that pitchers get to take entire games off. You'll have to practice your cheerleader pep talks."

Shaking his head, Skeet said to Finley, "Are you wondering what you got yourself into with a guy like Levi?"

She only smiled.

"All right, all right." Skeet lifted his hands. "I'm going to hit the shower. Meet you both in the parking lot in twenty?"

Levi looked down at Finley, who nodded. "See you then," Levi told Skeet.

After Skeet headed off the field, Levi asked Finley, "Are you sure? We don't have to go over to his place."

"It's fine," she said. "I didn't come to keep you away from all the activities. We could go to the team thing if you want instead."

"Um, no." Levi scanned her, liking what he saw. Finley wore jeans with small rips in them, and a Minnesota Ice V-neck jersey with his number on it. "Did I tell you I like you in this outfit?"

Her cheeks dimpled. "More than once. Remember you made me try it on when you gave it to me?"

"I remember that well." He winked.

Finley's cheeks flushed pink. So he did what any sane boyfriend would do. He pulled her into his arms.

"Sorry, Mr. Florida," she said. "You're going to have to wait." She pushed against his chest with a coy smile. "Plus you're sweaty."

He scoffed, but she'd already stepped away.

"All right," he said. "I'm heading for the showers too."

"I'll wait by the exit to the parking lot," she said.

He watched her walk away, then pulled his distracted thoughts back into focus. Yeah, the win had been nice, but even better was that Finley was here.

Skeeter beat him to the parking lot, and when Levi stepped out of the exit, he slowed. Finley was walking with Skeeter around his restored Mustang.

Levi had seen it a few months ago when the Six Pack had all gone to Belltown for Mamma Sal's wedding. Levi hadn't known Skeeter had brought the Mustang to Columbus. Levi continued toward the dark-red car, admiring the deep cherry glowing beneath the parking lot lights and the polished rims adding to the stunning effect.

Levi might be surprised to see the Mustang here, but he was more surprised to see Finley's *I'm-in-love-with-this-car* smile.

"I didn't know you brought Ellie all the way out here," Levi said.

Finley looked over at Levi. "Who's Ellie?"

"That's her name," Skeeter answered. "She's a 1967 Fastback Eleanor."

Finley ran her hand over the hood. "Can I drive her?"

Levi fully expected Skeeter to say no, but he said, "I don't know. Can you?"

Finley smirked. "I learned to drive in a Mustang. My dad had one. It was nearly rusted through, but it ran."

"So, sort of like Levi's Bronco?" Skeeter teased.

"Whatever, man," Levi said. "The Bronco runs fine. And there's no rust."

Finley crossed to Levi and slipped her arm through his. Which made him pleased. "I like your Bronco fine, but this Mustang is something else. Even you can't deny that, Mr. Florida."

Skeet arched a brow, looking between the two of them.

"Fine," Levi said. "You guys win. My Bronco may not compare, but they are both loved."

Skeeter laughed and pulled a set of keys out of his jeans pocket. "She's all yours, Finley. But I'm sitting in the passenger seat."

Levi scowled; Skeet ignored him.

Finley released Levi's arm and took the keys from Skeeter. Once they were all inside, with Skeeter sitting in the front passenger seat, Finley started up Ellie. She rumbled to life and settled into a contented purr.

Skeeter guided Finley out of the parking lot, reminding Levi a bit of a parent teaching a fifteen-year-old to drive. But Finley only nodded at everything Skeeter said, a permanent grin on her face.

By the time they arrived at Skeeter's condo complex, Levi was duly impressed with Finley's driving. And he was reconsidering the car that he drove. Finley had never made such exclamations of joy when they were in his Bronco.

"Are you handy in the kitchen?" Skeeter asked Finley as they approached his condo door.

"I'm no gourmet chef, but I dare say I know a little more than Levi," she said, cutting him a smile.

"Good," Skeet said with a laugh. "I was hoping you'd say that. Maybe you and Levi can put together the veggies while I get the steaks on the grill."

"Veggies?" Levi said, following the two of them into the condo. "No chips?"

"Oh, I've got plenty of that too," Skeet said. "Have to keep the muscles healthy."

Levi had been to Skeeter's place before, but it had been a while. The place was full of furniture—well, not *full*, but furnished like most people's places. And Finley had noticed too.

She turned and waited for him, then linked their hands. Skeeter headed into the kitchen while they lingered in the living room.

Levi liked that she was taking this sort of initiative. Holding his hand, and other stuff.

"Don't say it," he told her, knowing she was about to comment on the presence of furniture in Skeeter's place.

She smirked. "Something to look forward to, right?"

He leaned down and almost kissed her, but she moved away, her brown eyes twinkling. "You need to work on your patience, Levi Cox."

He groaned, and she tugged him by the hand into the kitchen, where Skeeter had already taken some steaks out of the fridge. "A lot of seasoning, or a little?" he asked.

"Give me the Skeeter special," Levi said.

"As you wish." Skeeter threw a wink at Finley, and she winked back.

Levi frowned. Maybe he should have kept Finley to himself tonight.

Skeeter pointed Finley in the direction of salad fixings and tasked Levi with pouring chips into a plastic bowl. That right there told Levi where he was in the pecking order.

So after Levi finished his ten-second job, he made it his business to help Finley. Mostly by watching her chop up peppers and cucumbers and dice tomatoes.

Skeeter had left the sliding door open to the back patio, where he'd hooked up a music playlist to some outdoor speakers.

"You can help chop, you know," Finley said, pausing and eyeing Levi.

"I kind of like watching you work," he said, hiding a smile.

She shook her head and started on the lettuce.

Levi rose from the barstool and walked around the counter until he was standing behind her. He slipped his hands around her waist and put his hands on her hands.

"That's not helping," she said with a laugh.

So he wrapped her in his arms and pulled her against him.

Finley had no option but to pause in her work.

"That's better," Levi murmured, then pressed a kiss on her neck.

"Your friend can come in here at any second," Finley said, but she made no effort to disentangle herself.

"I don't care," Levi said, kissing her neck again and breathing in her raspberry scent.

Finley turned in his embrace, facing him, and looped her arms about his neck. He liked what he saw in her brown eyes—warmth and humor.

"You're not going to give up, are you?" she whispered.

He smiled. "Giving up's not in my nature."

She kissed him then, and he wished that Skeeter weren't on the other side of the wall, because Levi didn't want this kiss to end. He held her carefully because of her bruised ribs, even though she wasn't complaining.

Finley drew away much, much too soon. And it was then that Levi realized that Skeeter had come into the kitchen.

"We've got about fifteen minutes before the steaks are

done," he said. "How's the salad coming?" The laughter was unmistakable in his eyes.

"Almost done," Finley said in a perfectly even, normal tone.

Levi wasn't feeling so at ease himself. Maybe he should go help Skeeter with something while Finley finished the salad.

So he went out to the back patio with Skeeter.

"Smells good," Levi said, looking at the sizzling grill.

But when Skeeter didn't answer, Levi looked over at his friend.

Skeet had his arms folded, and he was pretty much staring Levi down.

"What?" Levi said.

"You'd better not screw this up."

"What? Finley?"

"Yeah," Skeeter said.

Levi couldn't decide if he was offended or if he was about to laugh. "What makes you say that I'd screw anything up? I like Finley. A lot. And I think I'm doing okay in the boyfriend department."

Skeeter reached for the barbeque tongs and flipped over the steaks one at a time. "I know how you can be, Steal. Cutting yourself off from everyone and everything. Going quiet on the Six Pack."

Levi exhaled. He wasn't really in the mood to have *this* talk. "Finley's different."

"I can see that," Skeeter said. "And I can see that you're different with her. Which is a good thing in my opinion." He looked up from the grill. "I'm letting you know that I have her back over yours."

Levi raised his brows. Okay, now he really was offended. But he was sort of proud of Skeeter too. Because anyone with a brain should take Finley Gray's side, no matter what. "What happened to our years of friendship? Our baseball-team bonding? The unbreakable Six Pack?"

Skeeter shrugged as if it were easy to dismiss their shared history. "I don't want to see you making the biggest mistake of your life."

Levi walked around the grill and leaned against the railing that joined up with a set of stairs. "Unless she dumps me, I'm not going anywhere."

Skeeter's brows lifted.

"I want more," Levi said, deciding to be more open than usual. "I know I can't push things too fast between us, but I know that Finley is the real deal. I want our futures to be together, and if she'll agree, we'll be business partners in the furniture restoration business."

Skeeter's mouth twitched.

"It's not funny."

"*You.* In the furniture business?" he asked.

Levi pulled out his phone and showed Skeeter his new couch, courtesy of Finley.

"I like it," Skeet said. "So what's the plan?"

"The plan is," Levi began, "to be an investor. She designs the furniture. I can help when I'm in town. She sells it, and no more waitressing at the pub."

Skeet nodded, a knowing look in his eyes. "She hasn't agreed yet, has she?"

Levi looked over the deck at the trees beyond and exhaled. "No."

"Then tell her how you feel," Skeet said.

Levi snapped his gaze to his friend. "You think that will do it?"

Skeeter grinned. "I have a good feeling that it will."

Levi's pulse had gone up more than a notch or two.

"Where do you want me to set the table?" Finley asked, coming to stand in the doorway of the sliding door.

"That's Levi's job," Skeeter said. "We can eat out here."

Levi headed into the kitchen and rifled through cupboards and drawers until he found everything. He could hear the rise and fall of Skeeter and Finley's voices outside.

Levi felt nervous for some reason. Because the conversation with Skeeter had made Levi wonder how early was too early to tell a woman that he was in love with her? And would confessing to Finley be what it took to convince her to leave that rathole pub and partner in business with him?

Yes, Levi agreed with Skeeter. Levi didn't want to screw any of this up. So, should he wait? Or confess?

"Steak's ready!" Skeeter hollered.

Levi gathered the last item—a roll of paper towels, because he hadn't been able to find any napkins. Then he carried everything outside.

Finley crossed over to him and took the paper towels, along with the cans of soda from the top of the pile that was about to tip over.

As they ate, Skeeter mostly asked Finley questions about living in Minnesota and boxing, and she seemed at ease to answer them.

Then Skeeter turned to Levi and said, "Any birthday plans next week?"

Levi about choked on the piece of steak he was chewing. He finished chewing and gave Skeeter a death glare.

Skeet only chuckled. "I don't get why you hate your birthday so much."

"It's your birthday next week?" Finley asked.

"Uh-oh," Skeet said, raising his hands. "I'll do the cleanup while you two work this one out."

Skeeter made fast work of picking up his plate and soda

can, then leaving the patio. Levi could feel Finley's gaze on him the entire time. When they were alone, Finley said, "Were you going to tell me any time soon?"

"No," Levi said, rubbing a hand over his face. "It's this Wednesday, and we're playing at home that night. Just another game. And Skeet's right. I don't care for my birthday."

"Why?" Finley said in a quiet voice.

Levi swallowed against the hard lump in his throat. Not even the Six Pack knew the real reason. But Finley was the woman he loved, right? And if they were to build a future together, he should be able to tell her. "The night of my seventh birthday was when my mom was arrested. I never saw her again."

CHAPTER 24

"Do you think Levi's going to hate me?" Finley asked Grizz over the phone.

"He'll be shocked, that's for sure." Grizz's voice rumbled through the phone. "But he'll get over it too."

Finley exhaled and closed her eyes. She was leaning against the wall near one of the stadium's snack booths during the fifth inning of the Wednesday night game. Levi's birthday, to be exact. She'd told him happy birthday earlier that day, and he'd said the standard thank you. It was a given they'd probably hang out after his game. They always did when she wasn't working, and even when she was, since he was still in the habit of showing up at the pub and driving her two blocks to her apartment.

"I'm picking up Rabbit and Rhett now at their terminal," Grizz said. "Be there soon."

"Okay." Finley hung up with Grizz, then sent Sawyer a text. *Everyone's on their way. Plan's moving ahead.*

Make sure you send me video, Skeet wrote back.

Finley smiled and wrote: *Will do. Thanks for all your help.*

No problem. He deserves something good, Skeet wrote. *But don't tell him I said that.*

She laughed. *Your secret is safe with me.*

It was time to head back to her seat. Levi would notice her absence if she was gone too long. That was just how he was. And she liked that about him. Levi hadn't pressured her any more about starting up a business, but she could tell that he was holding back his opinions. And trying not to push her too much.

Sometimes he treated her like she was a fragile thing who was about to break. She liked the protective side of him, but she'd been protected all her life by her dad. Her dad had always put her first, always taken care of her. And she could see the same thing in Levi.

That was why she'd called Skeeter yesterday after getting to know him better in Ohio over the weekend, and together they'd come up with a pretty wild plan.

Finley rejoined her dad in their reserved seats, courtesy of Levi, of course.

"They're coming?" her dad said.

"Yep," Finley said, feeling breathless. This was really happening. "Grizz is picking up Rabbit and Rhett right now."

Her dad nodded, then turned his focus back to the game. Minnesota Ice was up by one against Iowa Devils, but things were tense. Levi had already had words with the Devils' pitcher, Ramie.

Finley watched the rest of the fifth inning, and throughout the entire sixth inning, she was as nervous as a cat near a rocking chair.

When the text from Grizz came in at the beginning of the seventh inning, Finley felt like a weight had been lifted. "They're here," she told her dad.

He grinned and patted her arm. "Told you they'd make it."

Maybe Finley should have trusted in Levi's friends more. But asking Rabbit, Grizz, and Rhett to all fly in tonight at the last minute had been risky at best. Finley stayed in her seat. She knew that the guys would keep low until the right moment.

As for Finley, she gripped the edges of her seat, hoping that Levi would take the surprise in stride. She understood why he hated his birthday. But he had a lot of birthdays ahead of him, and Finley wanted to change his perception. Start anew.

The seventh inning started with Levi catching a foul ball that sailed to the side of his base. Finley cheered and wished she didn't have to sit back down. She would have rather paced and eased her nerves.

Big T was pitching, and he walked the next person.

Finley groaned with disappointment and hoped it wasn't a pattern.

"Come on, Big T!" her dad shouted. "Send him some ice!"

Big T struck the next batter out.

Finley leaned forward as another Devils batter walked up to the plate.

"Show 'im what you got, T!" Levi called out to his teammate. "Three strikes."

Two outs. One on base.

One more out, and it would be the seventh-inning stretch. When, Finley hoped, her plans would fall into place.

"Strike one!" the ump called.

Finley gripped her hands together, focusing on Big T's windup and subsequent pitch. Straight over the plate, level with the strike zone.

The batter swung too high.

"Strike two!"

Finley picked up the bouquet of red roses she'd placed under her seat, then she stood and walked to the aisle. Her dad followed, and they headed down the steps, toward the gate that led to the field.

Big T went into his windup and pitched.

"Strike three!"

The Minnesota Ice fans cheered. A relieved breath whooshed out of Finley. She and her dad reached the gate, and per Skeeter's connections, the security guard was in the loop. He nodded and opened the gate. Finley and her dad paused before walking onto the field. The players had already gone into their dugouts.

The announcer's voice echoed across the stadium as people stood and stretched or headed to get their final snacks of the night.

"Well, folks, we have a special song tonight for the seventh-inning stretch," the announcer said. "Instead of singing our national anthem, we'll be singing 'Happy Birthday' to our very own Levi Cox."

The crowd hushed as they realized the agenda had shifted.

Then, in his deep voice, the announcer began to sing "Happy Birthday." At that moment, Finley caught sight of Grizz, Rabbit, and Rhett coming through another gate. Rabbit waved at her, and Finley smiled.

She and her dad started walking toward the infield. Finley held up her phone, recording for Skeeter. They'd meet Rhett and the others at the pitcher's mound and sing with the crowd.

The birthday song grew louder as more fans joined in, and soon the entire stadium vibrated with voices singing to Levi.

Finley didn't dare look in the direction of the Ice dugout. Her heart was pounding so hard that she was sure if she found out that Levi was upset about this, her heart would completely stop. She handed her phone to her dad while it was recording, because her hands had started to tremble. "Take it."

Her dad took over the recording, and somehow she kept walking, kept singing, and it wasn't lost on her that she was gripping her dad's arm.

When she passed by third base, she let go of her dad's arm. She couldn't go any farther, because she'd seen Levi step out of the dugout. Her dad kept walking toward the pitcher's mound, where Grizz, Rabbit, Rhett, and now a half dozen Ice players stood, belting out the Happy Birthday song.

But Finley's gaze was locked with Levi's. He was staring at her, the look on his face incredulous. At least he wasn't frowning or scowling, but he wasn't exactly smiling either.

The song came to an end, but the crowd didn't stop. They began singing another round of the song, singing even louder, if that was possible. Levi broke his gaze from Finley and turned almost a full circle, surveying the singing baseball fans.

Then he saw his brother, her dad, then Grizz and Rabbit.

Finley couldn't even guess what was going through Levi's mind. He rubbed a hand over his face, as if he was trying to decide if this was all real. Her eyes burned with emotion. Still, she couldn't move from her spot near third base, the bouquet of roses gripped in her hand as if it were the only thing holding her up.

As the second round of the song came to an end, Levi was back to looking at her.

Then her heart nearly did stop, because he started walking toward her. Not going over to greet his teammates or even his brother. The crowd's singing turned to cheering, and

Finley took a shaky breath as she watched him approach, his dark-green eyes focused solely on her.

Levi's uniform was dirty from his base stealing, and he was probably sweaty to go along with that. He must have shaved earlier today, because his jaw was smooth. And suddenly he was there, in front of her.

"What did you do?" he asked, the edges of his voice raspy.

She held up the bouquet. "I brought you roses for your birthday. I hope you love flowers."

Levi blinked. He looked down at the roses, then back up at her. And then he cradled her face with his warm, strong hands and kissed her. Hard. In front of twenty-five thousand cheering fans.

Finley dropped the bouquet, wrapped her arms about his neck, and kissed him back. Levi slid his hands over her back, then lifted her against him.

Finley wondered if her feet would ever touch the ground again. Her heart was on the verge of leaping out of her chest and floating away. Levi's mouth was warm, his kissing urgent, and his hands kept her anchored to him. Finley wanted to laugh or cry, she wasn't sure which. Levi didn't hate her at all.

When he pulled away, it wasn't to release her. His gaze bore into hers, completely ignoring the stadium full of people.

"I love you, Finley Gray," he said.

She did laugh then. "You'd better."

Levi lifted a brow, but he was smiling. Waiting. Because of course he knew.

Finley smiled back at the man she'd fallen hard for. "I love you too, Levi Cox."

And . . . Levi kissed her again. This time they weren't the only ones on third base though.

"Some of us came a long way to see you, bro," Rhett said, clapping a hand on Levi's shoulder.

Levi finally released Finley and turned to greet his brother.

Finley blinked back tears as he questioned Grizz and Rabbit, asking how they all pulled this off.

"It was Finley," Grizz said, one eyebrow cocked above his aviator glasses. "She said to get on a plane, and here we are."

Levi shook his head, then pulled Finley against him and kissed her temple.

"Time's up," Rabbit said. "How about you win this one? Since you've got quite the audience."

Levi drew away from Finley, and it was all she could do to let him go. As Levi returned to the dugout, he raised his hand to the crowd in a sign of thanks. Then he got plenty of pats on the back and birthday wishes from his teammates.

"We need to leave the field," Grizz said, touching Finley's arm and bringing her back to the here and now.

"Oh, right," she said, her face heating up.

Grizz just smiled, and she walked with the group to the gate that led to the stands.

"I can't believe you pulled it off," Rhett said. "I should have brought Erin. She would have loved it."

Finley smiled. "I'm glad you could come."

As they made their way to their seats, both Grizz and Rabbit were stopped several times and asked for autographs.

Other fans shifted around so that the three newcomers could sit with Finley and her dad.

"You did good, kid," her dad said, giving her a half hug. "You sure surprised the hell outta him. I'll have to admit, it was fun to watch."

Finley smiled. She felt all jittery inside. First, because they *had* pulled it off. Second, because Levi hadn't been upset at all. And . . . he'd told her he loved her.

As the next innings played out, Finley was quiet, letting

her thoughts and emotions soak in, independent of what was going on around her.

Everything else became a blur because suddenly the relationship between her and Levi had become very, very clear.

But it wasn't for another few hours that Finley was able to have Levi to herself. After the game, after the congratulations on the win, after the dinner at an all-night breakfast joint, after saying goodbye to the guys and her dad, after she'd texted Mark at work, and after Levi drove her home. In his Bronco.

As Levi walked her up to her place, he held her fingers loosely, and Finley tried to figure out how to best tell him all the decisions she'd made in the last couple of hours.

"Coming in?" she said as they reached her door, and she pulled out her key.

"Is that an invitation?" Levi asked.

She smiled. "It is." She opened the door, and he followed her inside.

Her apartment was back to normal, at least for a few more days. She'd already scoped out the upcoming weekend's garage sales. She was even thinking of upping her game and registering to attend some estate sales. But that would depend on Levi's response to her plan.

"Your place looks almost bare now," Levi said.

"Thanks to you helping my dad clear all the stuff out," she said. "You know, you're the best sales guy I know."

"Oh really?" he crossed toward her, and she stepped back until she reached the kitchen table.

He leaned down, resting his hands on the table on either side of her. "If you didn't create good product, it wouldn't be so easy to sell."

She rested her hands on his solid chest, her right hand over his heart.

"I can't believe what you did tonight," he said, scanning her face. "I've never had anyone do something like that for me."

Finley moved her hands up to his shoulders. "I was worried you'd be mad at all the attention because you told me you hated your birthday."

Levi gazed at her for a moment. "I don't hate it any more. Thanks to you."

She smiled. "Good."

He lifted a hand and touched the edge of her jaw. "What ever happened to those roses?"

Finley opened her mouth, then closed it.

Levi chuckled. "I think Rhett ended up with them."

"I was sort of preoccupied, I guess." She moved her hands over his shoulders. "You know, I've been thinking . . ."

When she didn't continue, Levi leaned closer. "About how much you love me?"

Finley smiled. "Sort of."

He quirked a brow.

"About taking you up on your offer to go into business."

Levi drew away. "Really?"

"Really."

He pulled her against him into a tight bear hug.

Finley laughed. "So are you still offering, then?"

"Of course." He loosened his tight hold. "When are you quitting the pub?"

She drew away, keeping her arms looped around his neck. "I put in my two weeks' notice tonight."

"Did I tell you that I love you?" he said in a low voice.

Goose bumps raced across her skin. "Um, you did while kissing me on third."

Levi smiled.

"And I have one more thing to tell you," she said, running her hand over his bicep and down his arm.

He kissed her forehead. "How many surprises do you have for me?"

"This is the last one." She continued to trail her hand along his forearm, then his wrist, and finally linked fingers with him. "That last match against Shirley Temple might have been my last one."

Levi stilled. "When did you decide that?"

"I don't know exactly," Finley said, looking down at their clasped hands. "I'm still thinking about it, but I don't really have the desire anymore."

"Because I fulfill all your needs and desires?" he teased.

She looked up at him to see the glint in his dark-green eyes. "You're not getting that much credit."

His smile was soft. "Whatever you want to do, I'll be there."

"I know," she whispered. She leaned against him, wrapping her arms about his waist. The thump of his heart sounded next to her ear. Maybe Levi could take the credit. Because he'd definitely become her happy place.

His hands moved up her back in a slow caress. "Get your laptop," he said. "We have a business plan to write."

Finley closed her eyes, not wanting to release him yet. "Tomorrow," she said.

"Okay, boss."

She lifted her head and gazed at him. "So now I'm your boss?"

"Yep." He winked. "I'm the lowly investor, remember? Although I plan on keeping you in line at all times."

Finley smirked. "Okay, Mr. Florida. You can start by kissing me again."

Levi grinned and did just that.

More #Belltown Six Pack Novels

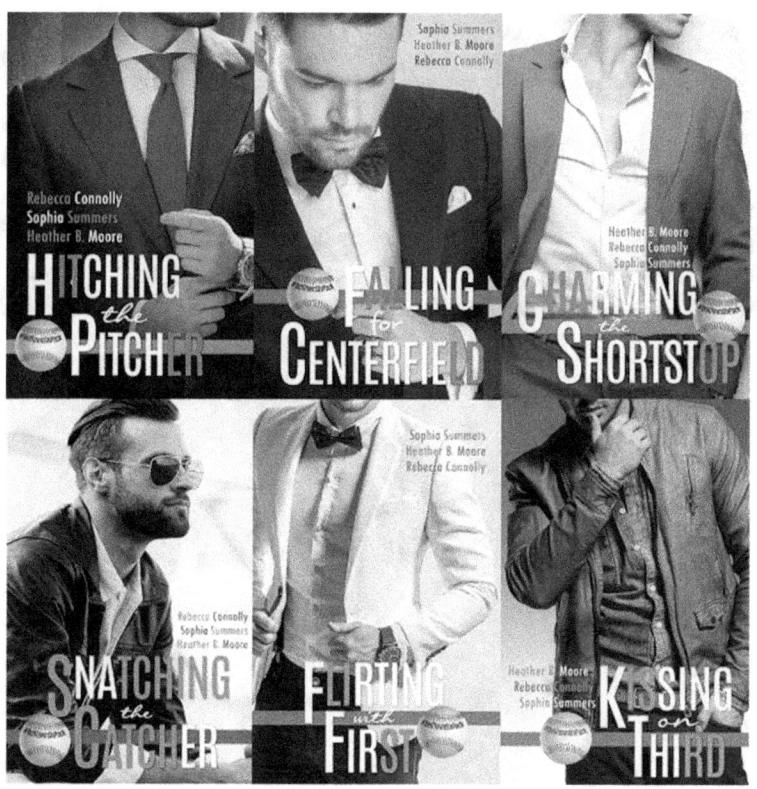

JOIN US ON FACEBOOK: SWOONY SPORTS ROMANCES

Heather B. Moore is a four-time *USA Today* bestselling author. She writes historical thrillers under the pen name H.B. Moore; her latest thrillers include *The Killing Curse* and *Breaking Jess*. Under the name Heather B. Moore, she writes romance and women's fiction. Her newest releases include the historical romances *Love is Come* and *Ruth*. She's also one of the coauthors of the *USA Today* bestselling series: A Timeless Romance Anthology. Heather writes speculative fiction under the pen name Jane Redd; releases include the Solstice series and *Mistress Grim*. Heather is represented by Dystel, Goderich & Bourret.

For book updates, sign up for Heather's email list: hbmoore.com/contact
    Website: HBMoore.com
    Facebook: Fans of H. B. Moore
    Blog: MyWritersLair.blogspot.com
    Instagram: @authorhbmoore
    Twitter: @HeatherBMoore

www.ingramcontent.com/pod-product-compliance
Lightning Source LLC
LaVergne TN
LVHW021811060526
838201LV00058B/3325